HOMETOWN HERO

"I'm so glad you're finally realizing how wonderful Don is," Danielle said smugly. "In fact, I think I'll even let each of you dance with him at the Sadie Hawkins Ball. But only one dance each."

Ashley sat straight up and shot Wendy a look. "Sadie Hawkins! You can't tell me he's *your* date! I'm going to ask him to the dance!"

"Well, I plan to ask him, too!" Wendy cried.

Danielle shook her head in disbelief. If either of those two thought they were going to get their paws on Don before she did, they were vastly underrating the cunning of Danielle Sharp!

Merivale Mall

HOMETOWN HERO

by Jana Ellis

Troll Associates

Library of Congress Cataloging-in-Publication Data

Ellis, Jana.
   Hometown hero / by Jana Ellis.
     p.   cm.—(Merivale mall , #7)
   Summary: Rich snob Danielle is ashamed to be seen at the mall
with attractive but poor Don, until he saves a child's life and
becomes the town hero; then she is tempted to abandon him when he is
connected with burglaries at the mall.
   ISBN 0-8167-1609-9 (pbk)
   [1. Heroes—Fiction. 2. Popularity—Fiction. 3 Shopping malls—
Fiction.] I. Title. II. Series: Ellis, Jana. Merivale mall ; #7
PZ7.E472Ho 1990
[Fic]—dc20   .   89-34374

A TROLL BOOK, published by Troll Associates,
Mahwah, NJ 07430

Printed in the United States of America.

10 9 8 7 6 5 4 3 2 1

CHAPTER ONE

"Will you guys lay off? I've said it a thousand times, and I'll say it again—I wouldn't ask Don James to the Sadie Hawkins dance if my life depended on it!"

Sixteen-year-old Danielle Sharp tossed her fiery red hair as she flashed a defiant glance at her two best friends, Teresa Woods and Heather Barron.

"I know you wouldn't *really* ask him," said Teresa. "But you'd *like* to, wouldn't you? You can be honest with me, Danielle."

"I would *not* like to!" Danielle declared.

"Sure, sure—" murmured Heather sarcastically.

Sometimes, Heather Barron and Teresa Woods could be real pains. There they were at Merivale Mall, shopping in Facades, their favorite boutique. They were surrounded by all the gorgeous new spring fashions in fantasy pastel

1

colors, and the only thing Heather and Teresa could talk about was Don James!

Danielle had been caught dating Don only one time. Of course, she had been with him a few other times—but on the sly. Unfortunately, the one time she had been seen with him was recorded for posterity by Jane Haggerty and her world-class mouth. After that Danielle had been ultra careful not to go out in public with Don. And recently she had decided to give him up completely.

Listening to her friends had brought her to the sad conclusion that maybe they were right, Don James just wasn't good enough for her. For starters, he was poor. Don lived in a run-down farmhouse with a bunch of guys outside of town. He worked part-time as a car mechanic when he wasn't in school at Merivale High. Danielle's friends could not accept her going out with someone so low class. And that meant, no matter how much she liked him, how gorgeous he was, she was determined *never* to go out with Don James again.

"I haven't even spoken two words to him in weeks, and I certainly don't intend to start now," she insisted, fingering the label on a pair of gray silk slacks.

"Oh, come on, Danielle," drawled Teresa, crinkling her turned-up nose and winking a chocolate-brown eye. "We can tell by the way you look at him. Every time you see him in the

Video Arcade, you practically start panting. Face it, you can't fool your best friends. We *know* you'd love to ask him to the dance!"

"Really, Danielle," echoed Heather, drawing her professionally manicured fingers through her shiny raven hair and batting her ice-blue eyes. "I mean, I can understand if you bring Don James. Just be sure you bring a towel to wipe off the axle grease!"

Her friends burst into giggles, and Danielle smiled, but inside she was fuming. Don might study auto mechanics at school, but he always cleaned up for her.

But most important, Don was a really sweet guy. Aside from his incredible good looks, he had a great sense of humor and he was always ready to help a friend, which was more than Danielle could say about Teresa or Heather.

But what got to Danielle the most was that Teresa and Heather were one hundred percent right about the way she felt about Don. She really *did* want to ask him to the Sadie Hawkins dance. She'd been daydreaming about it for weeks, ever since the dance had been announced.

Still, she'd never do it. If she walked into Atwood Academy on Don James's arm, her crowd would never forgive her. They just didn't accept people who were different, and Don was *beyond* different. Besides, the Sadie Hawkins dance was formal, and Don would never wear a tuxedo. That just wasn't his style.

Miserably, Danielle plucked a pink silk blouse off the rack and then put it right back. *Why can't you just forget him?* she thought.

Then, hoping to distract her friends, she sauntered over to a standing rack of lightweight suede jackets. "Ooh! Check these out! Did you ever see such fabulous colors?"

Teresa and Heather stepped over to the rack, still wearing their annoying smug grins. "Not bad," said Heather, taking one off the rack and holding it up in front of her. "I like it, actually."

"Yeah," agreed Teresa, taking another. "Oh, Danielle! Hold this red one up to you! I want to see if it clashes with your hair."

At last . . . Maybe her friends had finally gotten off Don James. It was amazing what clothes could do to Heather and Teresa. If Earth was ever invaded by creatures from outer space, all Heather and Teresa would care about was what the aliens were wearing.

With a small smile, Danielle picked up the red jacket and froze. Behind the rack of suedes, two wide hazel eyes darted away as she looked up. Someone was trying to avoid her.

Pushing all the jackets aside, Danielle found herself staring at Jane Haggerty. Obviously Atwood Academy's gossip supreme had been listening to every word of Danielle and her friends.

Danielle blushed to her roots. If Jane heard

all that stuff about her and Don James, she'd start the gossip about them all over again.

"Well, hello, hello. If it isn't Janey," Danielle said in as unconcerned a manner as she could manage. "I suppose you were just looking for something suede, and couldn't help over-hearing—"

Jane didn't even bother to deny it. "So, Danielle, if not Don James, who's it going to be? Come on, tell all!"

"I know! Keith Canfield!" said Heather, a mischievous twinkle in her eyes as she looked up at Danielle.

That comment sent Teresa and Heather into gales of laughter. Earlier that year, Danielle had developed just the teensiest crush on Keith—he *was* a hunk after all. He had the longest lashes and the most fantastic blue eyes. But she'd found out he was more interested in insects and bugs than in girls and tell-all Jane would never let her live that one down either.

But Danielle Sharp was not to be toyed with or tormented. "My dear friends," she said, smirking. "How come it's always *me* all Merivale's dying to know about? Why don't you tell us who *you'd* like to ask, Jane?"

Ah-ha! A blush from Jane told Danielle that whoever it was, Jane didn't want anybody to know. But Danielle's little trick had worked. All eyes were on Jane now, and off *her*.

"It's hard to choose," Jane lied. She'd have

a hard time finding anyone who'd go with her. "How about you, Heather? Is Rob Matthews the lucky guy?"

"I've asked him. And yes, he's already agreed," replied Heather.

"You, Teresa?" Jane asked.

Standing in front of an antique glass mirror, Teresa held a delicious pink dress in front of her and swayed back and forth. "For me to know and you to find out, Jane," she said with a smile. "I can tell you this. He's someone incredible, and he'll be at the big party after the dance. I mean, everybody's going to be there—everybody who's anybody, that is."

Danielle took a deep breath as Heather and Teresa and Jane started talking about the dance. Sometimes being an Atwood girl was hard, what with appearances to keep up and the worry about what everyone else thought. . . .

Danielle still wasn't used to it, even after three years of being rich. When she was growing up, her family had been no better off than most families in town. But then her father got his big break, designing Merivale Mall. The Sharps moved to Wood Hollow Hills, and Danielle started at Atwood Academy, the most prestigious and exclusive private school in the area.

It was all wonderful, Danielle knew, but sometimes, it was a real strain. . . .

"Here we are, Pats. What's the emergency?" Lori Randall said, trotting up to the counter of the Cookie Connection, her blond hair flying behind her. The smell of freshly baked chocolate-chip cookies hung heavy in the air, and Lori took a deep breath and savored the rich aroma.

Right behind Lori was Ann Larson. Gray-eyed, brown-haired Ann worked as an aerobics instructor at the Body Shoppe, the mall's exercise spa, after school and on weekends. She was definitely one of the healthiest people in Merivale, or anywhere. She and Lori and Patsy Donovan were all juniors at Merivale High. They were also the three best friends in the entire universe.

Hazel-eyed Patsy looked up and tilted her head, sending her reddish-brown curls to one side. The big cookie-shaped hat on her head flopped over too. "Thanks for coming, you two," she said, and sighed.

At the moment Patsy looked truly pathetic. Her silly Cookie Connection uniform just didn't go with the desperate look on her face. "It's really bad, guys—"

"Patsy!" called her boss, Joe Murphy, from the back of the store. "It's time for your break, unless you aren't taking one." Good old Joe knew something was going on with Patsy and that she needed to talk to her friends.

"Thanks, Murph," said Patsy, moving around the counter to meet her friends. "Come on," she said, leading them past a display of cinnamon croissants and out the door to an empty table in the main atrium of the mall. "I'll tell you everything."

"Out with it!" said Lori as they sat down at a small, round table. A few shoppers strolled by, window-shopping, but the mall was never very crowded this early. "It must be pretty serious, the way you sounded over the phone."

Patsy dropped her head and groaned. "It's Irv. He doesn't like me anymore."

Lori looked at her friend skeptically. "Irv? Not like you?" Irv Zalaznick, a fellow junior at Merivale High, was Patsy's lab partner. They'd been friends since their freshman year. In the past few weeks the friendship had blossomed into romance, and the two had been more or less going steady.

"He's completely rejecting me," Patsy announced dolefully.

"Patsy," said an incredulous Lori. "Irv Zalaznick practically worships at your feet!"

"I saw you together just before work, and he was looking at you as if you were a movie star!" Ann piped up.

"Oh, yeah? Then tell me this—how come he's stopped kissing me? He always used to, and suddenly he's stopped. It started last Friday, and I told myself it didn't mean anything, maybe he just wasn't in the mood or something. But then the last couple of days when he walked me to work—nothing!"

"Maybe he was just embarrassed to kiss you right here in the mall, Patsy," Ann suggested.

"But there wasn't anybody around, Ann," Patsy sputtered. "The place was practically empty. And besides, he always *used* to kiss me when he walked me to work! Today he just said, 'Well, so long, Pats,' and sort of punched my shoulder. It was really weird. I mean, what's happening to my big romance? You've got to tell me what I'm doing wrong!"

Lori and Ann exchanged a look. Irv Zalaznick was a great guy, but he didn't exactly have a reputation for being a Romeo. In fact, he was such a whiz at computers and science and math that lots of kids thought of him as a nerd, which wasn't true at all.

"Are you sure he's not mad at you for anything?" Lori asked gently.

"I don't think so, Lor. On the way over he told me I was the only girl he ever really liked and how he was happy that we were going out. And then we made plans for Friday night."

"That doesn't sound like a guy who's holding a grudge about anything," said Lori thoughtfully. "Well, have you asked him why?"

"*Asked* him? You mean, say, 'Hey, Irv. Why have you stopped kissing me?' " Patsy looked thoroughly shocked.

"You could try it," answered Lori.

"That way you won't have to guess. You'll know," said Ann.

"And if something is wrong, you can work on it," Lori added levelly.

But Patsy shook her head vigorously. "No way! I'd die of embarrassment!"

"I have an idea," suggested Lori. "Maybe you can do something really romantic together next time you go out. You could tell him you want to take a long walk, and then you could lead him to someplace really private—"

"Like the duck pond! That's the perfect place for romance," Ann chimed in.

"Then *you* can kiss *him* and see how he responds," added Lori.

"Me? Kiss him? Oh, no!" cried Patsy. "That's too aggressive!"

"Well, Patsy, one of you has to break the ice. Maybe he thinks you don't want him to kiss you anymore," said Lori.

"Why would he think that?" Patsy asked almost testily.

"Guys are funny sometimes, Patsy. Maybe you said something that he took the wrong way," Ann threw in.

"But I love it when he's romantic," Patsy protested.

"Speaking of romance—" Ann gently poked Lori in the ribs with her elbow and looked out across the mall.

There, in his blue and white Atwood Academy letter jacket, was Nick Hobart, Lori's boyfriend. The blond highlights in Nick's light brown hair were shining as he headed for his dad's store, Hobart Electronics. He looked relaxed and together as usual.

"Hi, Nick!" Lori called out. Nick turned, searching the area with his aquamarine eyes. When he saw the girls and focused in on Lori, he broke into a smile that made Lori's heart skip a beat.

"Don't say anything about me and Irv, okay, Lor?" Patsy muttered anxiously. "It's all so embarrassing."

"Of course not, Pats," Lori promised before turning to greet Nick with a big smile. Sometimes she couldn't believe she had such a great boyfriend. Nick was handsome, loyal, bright, and funny. And best of all, he was crazy about her! Ever since they had met, Lori was happier than she'd ever been.

"Hi!" said Nick brightly as he approached their table. Then he leaned over and planted a quick but loving kiss on Lori's cheek. "I see you're all hard at work," he teased.

The girls giggled, and Nick pulled up a chair from the table behind them.

"So, Nick, how are you?" asked Lori.

Nick shrugged. "I'm okay, but these robberies are really a drag. My dad's expecting a big shipment in a few days, and he's worried that he might lose everything."

"What robberies?" asked Lori.

"Haven't you heard?" said Ann. "That's why they've been putting in a closed circuit video system. It's going to be working tomorrow."

"There's a gang of thieves taking things from the loading docks after the stores close," Nick explained. "Two stores were practically wiped out a few days ago."

"Gosh," murmured Lori. "That's awful."

"Oh, no!" cried Ann, suddenly glancing up at a clock on one of the pillars. "My next class starts in three minutes!"

"Yikes, I've got to go too!" said Lori, quickly standing up and grabbing her sweater from the back of her chair.

"Me too," said Patsy, setting her chocolate-chip-cookie hat straight on her head again.

"Lori, can I walk you back to Tio's?" asked Nick in a way that made Lori melt. Nick was a gentleman through and through.

"Sure," Lori answered warmly. "See you guys," she said to her friends.

"Bye, and thanks, you two," Patsy told Lori and Ann. "I *feel* better about things now anyway."

Nick shot a confused look at Lori, who nodded in a way that made him know not to ask.

"Good," said Lori. "See you." With a wave, Lori and Nick walked away from their friends. Nick took her hand, and Lori felt a surge of heat shoot through her.

"Ahem," said Nick, clearing his throat as they passed Merivale Drugs heading for Tio's. "Lori, did you know we're having a Sadie Hawkins dance at Atwood a week from Saturday? It's a benefit for the children's hospital, and see, the girl is supposed to ask the guy, but since you don't go to Atwood, I thought maybe I'd ask you to—you know—ask me."

Nick gave a little laugh and squeezed her hand. "What do you say? Do I have a chance?"

Lori grinned. He always made her feel so special, and now he was pretending she might not ask him. He knew she'd been wanting to go to the biggest social event at Atwood all year.

When Nick, Atwood's star quarterback and number-one hunk, had started going out with Lori, a girl from lowly Merivale High, every red-blooded Atwood girl went through the roof—especially Lori's cousin Danielle. A lot of them still hadn't given up hoping Nick would change his mind about dating Lori.

"Well, I hate to break those Atwood girls' hearts, but consider yourself invited," said Lori.

"Thanks, Lor." He laughed and wiped his brow dramatically.

They were in front of Tio's now, but Lori still had one minute of her break left. No way was she going to cut it short.

"There's a party at Rob Matthews's house after the dance. Could you try to convince your folks to extend your curfew?" he asked, his hand still in hers.

Lori winced. "I'll try. But they've really been on my case since we got home so late that time."

"Hey, can I help it if being with you makes time stand still?" He grinned and stared deeply into her blue eyes. "Oh, Lori," he said, sighing happily. Then he bent down and gave her the sweetest kiss ever. And Lori almost forgot to breathe.

CHAPTER TWO

Ka-pow! Bleep! Bleep! Bleep! The next day Don James peered at the Star Command video game with a smile of triumph. He had just blasted his last megatron and racked up a five-hundred-point bonus on his total score.

The screen flashed his code name, Hubba, and blinked his total score—eleven thousand four hundred and seventy-five. According to the screen, only one other player had ever done better at a game of Star Command at the mall. His code name was Tron, and he held the record with twelve thousand three hundred and twenty points.

Move over, Tron baby! Don could smell an exciting victory coming. He was hot now. The next game could put him over the top—way beyond Tron's record. Just a little extra speed and he'd have a place in electronic history.

Reaching into his pocket, Don pulled out

two quarters and jammed them into the machine. His rugged, handsome face was a study of concentration as the new game came onscreen. Instantly his hands took hold of the joy stick and began blasting every target in sight.

Ka-pow! Bleep! An asteroid destroyed. *Ka-pow! Bleep! Bleep!* Two alien star ships shot to smithereens. *Erg.* One of his men took a hit. No big deal—it was still early in the game.

His strong hands on the firing controls, Don focused all his attention on the video screen. He knew he had to be totally there if he was going to win at Star Command. But a hand on his shoulder broke the mood.

"Don James? Got a minute?" a gruff voice asked.

Just then a megatron got Don's suprablaster. *Erg.* Another loss. Turning his head, he found himself looking straight into the cool brown eyes of Archie Tripp, the head of security at Merivale Mall. Tripp was wearing a gray security uniform and holding a walkie-talkie. Behind him stood nineteen-year-old Vince Tripp, Archie's son, who also worked as a security guard at the mall.

"Hi, Archie. What's up?" asked Don. Even though he hadn't done anything wrong, a shot of panic went through him. Archie Tripp wasn't known for being friendly.

"Just a few questions, Don. Vince here tells me that you spend a lot of time at the mall," the older man growled. "Is that right?"

Erg. There was no sense even trying to win the game anymore. With a shake of his glossy black hair, Don zapped one last megatron and turned around to face the two men.

"Yeah, I guess you could say that," Don answered as noncommittally as he could. He shot a quick, questioning look at Vince, who glanced away.

"Well, you probably know then," Tripp senior went on, "that we've been having a little problem here at the mall."

Don waited for the older man to say more, but he didn't. Instead, he drilled his brown eyes into Don's equally dark ones.

"Yeah?" said Don, who didn't know what else to say.

"Yeah," snapped Tripp. "Actually, this trouble is not so little. It has to do with the loading docks. Seems some people have been taking goods off the delivery trucks that park there overnight. The merchants have lost a fortune already." Tripp was looking at Don as if he were waiting for an answer.

"So? What's that got to do with me?" Don's heart was beating a mile a minute, even though he knew there was no reason for him to be afraid. Still, being hassled always made Don nervous.

"You ever go down to the loading docks?" Tripp was leaning on the Star Command machine now, his beefy form set in an overly casual posture.

"Sometimes," Don answered truthfully, shifting his weight to his left foot and away from Archie Tripp.

"Oh, you do? Now, that's interesting. And when was the last time you were down there?"

"I forget. Sometimes I use the lower level as a short cut to the other side of the parking lot. I usually park there." *What's this about?* Don wondered.

"A motorcycle?" Tripp asked.

"Yeah," Don answered. "And I've got an old white T-bird too."

"Tell me something else, Don—how's a kid like you get a motorcycle and a car?" Tripp was leaning in close now with an ugly frown.

Something in the way he was asking his questions sounded like an accusation. Don couldn't be positive, but he knew he didn't like the tone Archie was taking with him.

"What do you mean, how did I get a car and bike? I bought them, just like everyone else," answered Don.

"Yes, but that's pretty expensive for a kid on his own, isn't it?"

Don felt a surge of hot blood rise to his face. "I work over at Marty Taylor's garage on weekends and sometimes after school. I saved my money! And besides that, Marty got me good deals." Was Tripp implying that Don had stolen the Harley and the Bird he'd saved up for for months?

"Okay. Okay. Let's go over this again. You say you go down to the loading docks when you take a short cut—" There was something smug in Tripp's voice. "And when was the last time you went to the loading docks? It didn't happen to be a couple of nights ago, did it?"

Don could feel the pulse in his neck jumping at about ninety miles an hour. "Actually, I think I was around here a couple of nights ago. I might have used the lower level—I'm not really sure." That was the truth. Don had been so flustered about running into Danielle Sharp that night, he hadn't been thinking straight. Danielle had been about as warm as an iceberg to him.

"Very interesting," Tripp growled. "Because a couple of nights ago was the biggest heist yet. Whoever was down there cleared out over thirty thousand dollars worth of goods."

Don stared back at the older man in disbelief. Archie Tripp was practically accusing him of being a thief, and even though the whole idea was stupid, it could mean big trouble for Don.

"What's that got to do with me?" Don asked even though the answer was becoming painfully obvious.

"I'll level with you, Don. I think you're in with the thieves. *That's* what it's got to do with you." There wasn't much doubt in Tripp's voice either.

"Hold on a minute. You're talking to the

wrong guy—" Don's steady gaze was aimed straight at the mall's chief of security now. "You can't go around accusing people without proof! I'm not a thief—never have been!"

"I don't believe you, Don," Tripp grunted. "I think you're their lookout. We know they have one because there's no way our guards could be missing an operation like this without one. Come on. Level with me. Who're you working with?"

Don nervously raked a hand through his hair. "Nobody—that's who! I'm telling you, I don't know a thing about it." Throwing the security chief an icy glare, Don picked up his black leather jacket and hooked it over his shoulder as he started to walk away.

That's when Vince caught him by the shoulder and pulled him back. "My father is talking to you, turkey, and you'd better listen."

Vince Tripp never was big on brains, Don knew, but that didn't give him the right to push people around.

"Let go," Don muttered coolly. He shrugged and took a step away.

This time Vince grabbed Don's collar. But his father barked, "Let him go, Vince."

With a murderous look, Vince reluctantly released Don.

The older man walked up to Don and wagged his finger in his face. "I'll be watching you, Donnie boy. So don't try anything funny. Come on, Vince."

Shaken, Don watched Tripp and Vince walk out of Video Arcade. When they were far enough away, he stepped out into the mall and headed for the nearest exit. There was no sense hanging around now.

Walking past shoppers who were browsing, Don tried to sort everything out. One thing was sure—tonight he would definitely *not* take the short cut underground. That was over.

Don shook his head and exhaled hard. His whole life, it had always been the same. At the first sign of trouble, people always came running after Don James. Why? Had he ever done anything so terrible? His worst crime was skipping school, and he hadn't even done that after he'd gotten to high school and got turned on to auto mechanics.

But something always seemed to give people the wrong impression of him. Don couldn't help thinking it was just that he was different from other kids. Maybe it was because he didn't grow up in a regular family.

Or maybe it was because he dressed the way he did. Since he was a kid, the only pants he really liked to wear were jeans. His hair was a little longer than most guys, too, but he liked it that way. But wearing jeans and having long hair didn't make him a thief!

"No! No! Eddie—don't!" Above him a woman's panicked voice broke into Don's troubled thoughts. Looking up in the direction of the voice, he gasped. There was a baby about two years old, running beside the bars of the polished bronze railing on the next level. Suddenly the child sat down and stuck both his legs through space between the bars and began kicking. If he moved one inch forward, that kid was going to take a mighty big dive!

"Eddie! Eddie! Somebody help!" The mother's frantic cry echoed up and down the mall as she tore along trying to reach her child. But it was too late—the toddler's body slipped through the bars, falling toward the marble floor below!

CHAPTER THREE

Don leapt into action instantly. He raced toward the spot directly beneath the baby as the mother's frantic cries turned into screams.

Don's sneakers pounded across the tiled floor. In the next instant he felt the weight of the child dropping into his arms. Then, he fell too. Twisting impossibly, he rolled sideways as he landed, so that his shoulder, not the baby's head, connected with the hard floor.

Ouch! Don felt a searing pain spread through his shoulder as he landed. The frightened child let out a wail for his mother.

And there was another sound too. Cheering. Feeling dazed, Don looked up. A circle of bystanders had surrounded him and his precious charge and they were clapping.

"Bravo!" one older man cried.

"Unbelievable!" another woman shouted. "You saved that baby's life!"

Slowly a grin spread over Don's face. He felt like a hero—and in fact, he was one! While all those people had stood around, helpless, he had done something. And this little boy was alive because of it!

"It's okay, kid, it's okay," he said, happily patting the wailing child's head.

"Eddie! You're alive! You're alive!" The mother's jubilant cries were mixed with sobs as she rushed down the glass steps to her crying baby. "How can I ever thank you?" she sputtered at Don as she clasped her baby in her arms.

"Somebody help the hero up!" said an old man from the back of the gathering crowd.

"It's okay. I'm all right," said Don, cheerfully staggering to his feet as a few people tried to help him.

"Thank goodness! Oh, thank you so much!" the mother said, wiping away tears of panic and relief. "You saved my baby's life!"

Baby Eddie was more comfortable now. He pointed to Don with a huge smile that made everybody laugh with relief.

But just then Don felt a searing pain in his shoulder. Someone was grabbing him right in the spot that was tender from the fall.

"Archie Tripp?" asked Don, spinning around and facing the burly older man who'd just pushed his way through the crowd.

"What's going on here? Is there any problem?" Archie asked the baby's mother.

"This fellow caught my baby when he slipped through the railing. He saved Eddie's life!" Laughing between her tears, she pointed up to the place where her baby had fallen.

"That kid's a real hero!" said someone in the crowd.

"That was some terrific catch!" yelled someone else.

"I saw it! The baby was headed straight for the floor!" someone else spoke up.

"God bless him! He saved the baby. Good work, son!" the old man in the back cheered. And with that, the whole group burst into applause again.

"Well, does anybody want to fill out an accident form?" Tripp mumbled.

"Are you *sure* you're okay?" asked the baby's mother, ignoring Tripp.

"I'm okay," Don answered, rubbing his shoulder a little. "But I better get going now."

People started crowding around Don, reaching out to shake his hand or touch him lightly on the arm.

"The mayor should hear about this!" a man said, congratulating him.

"It's a pleasure to know there're young people like you," an older lady murmured.

"Thanks," said Don without a lot of self-importance.

Then he stepped confidently past Archie Tripp, a triumphant smile on his lips. Maybe this would prove to people what kind of a person Don James really was!

The next day Danielle's table in the Atwood cafeteria was overcrowded. Some girls had even squeezed in a few extra chairs, and the table was piled high with sandwich wrappers and soda cans. At the head of the table sat Danielle, basking in all the glory of being the girl who knew Don best.

"He really did look fantastic on TV, didn't he?" said Heather Barron with uncharacteristic enthusiasm.

"Yes!" agreed Wendy Carter, running a hand through her blunt-cut dark hair. "And wasn't it great the way the mall's new security TV system got the whole thing on tape?"

"It was on the radio too. They interviewed the baby's mother," Georgia Ross threw in. "She said Don was incredibly fast, and strong."

"Oh, and he's so *beautiful!*" Blond Ashley Shepard picked up the copy of the Merivale *Mirror* with Don's picture plastered all over it, and looked longingly at it.

"Well, this isn't public information yet," murmured Danielle, feeling smug, "but my father told me that the mayor and the mall association are going to have an award ceremony for Don. They're going to give him the key to the city—and some money."

"Wow," exclaimed Wendy, obviously impressed.

"Don James, a hero," said Jane Haggerty between bites of her watercress sandwich. "Who would've thought it?"

"Well, he still is who he is. If you know what I mean," said Teresa Woods, arching an eyebrow.

"No. What do you mean?" asked Danielle with a perplexed look.

"I mean, he's still low class," Teresa replied simply, before taking a bite of her cheese and cracker.

"That's true—but so what? Not all great people are born rich, Teresa," offered Heather Barron, the richest girl in Merivale. Danielle had to smile. This was a whole new side of Heather.

"Well, I think it's fine for other people, but I wouldn't go out with him," murmured Teresa.

"I would!" cried Wendy Carter, whose father was even richer than Teresa's. "I've *always* thought he was totally fab. And he's smart too."

Ha! That's a laugh, thought Danielle, rolling her eyes. Wendy Carter was always saying how dumb Don was. He only wanted to be a car mechanic. It was amazing how fickle some people could be.

"I've always thought he was fantastic too," Ashley piped up. "He's smart, and he's incredibly gorgeous! I love those rugged types."

"Like Hume Hargrove, for instance?" asked Danielle sarcastically. Hume was a real blueblood, and everyone at Atwood knew Ashley'd had a crush on him since day one. Trotting around on a polo pony was more Hume's style than riding a motorcycle.

The mere thought of Ashley Shepard or Wendy Carter or *any* of the girls at that table with somebody as down-to-earth as Don James made Danielle want to burst into uncontrollable giggles.

But Ashley and Wendy were serious about wanting to go out with Don. And they weren't the only ones. Every girl at Atwood seemed to have caught Don James fever.

Danielle, who had always tried to keep her attraction to Don a secret, couldn't help feeling a rush of superiority. After all, she had liked Don long before he became a hero. And now, at last, she wouldn't have to keep it a secret anymore. She could finally date him openly— and be admired for it!

"I'm so glad you are finally realizing just how wonderful Don is. In fact, I'll even let each of you dance with him at Sadie Hawkins. But only one dance each," said Danielle smugly.

Ashley sat up straight and shot Wendy a look. "Sadie Hawkins! You can't ask him to Sadie Hawkins, Danielle! I'm going to ask him to the dance."

"Well, I plan to ask him too!" Wendy cried.

Ashley was furious. "I just said I was going to ask him!"

"So what? Maybe he'd rather go with me!" Wendy declared. "We can both ask him and give him a choice. Well, bye, girls!"

Danielle shook her head in disbelief as she watched Wendy and the others begin to trickle out of the cafeteria.

"Good luck, Danielle," said Teresa, standing up and picking up her purse and books.

"See you later," said Danielle as casually as she could. Thank goodness Teresa and Heather weren't after Don too. Teresa was just too snobby, and Heather was hung up on Rob Matthews. But as for Ashley and Wendy—grrrrr. If either of those two thought they were going to get their paws on Don before *she* did, they were vastly underrating Danielle Sharp.

Danielle watched the cafeteria doors as the last of her friends pushed through them. She thought about Wendy and Ashley. The only thing those two had going for them were looks. In fact, it was kind of hard to think of any red-blooded male turning down either of them— even Don James!

Still, Danielle reminded herself, she had been there first. Why, she and Don James had liked each other since the day they were assigned seats next to each other in the sixth grade! Don had been crazy about her since then. Always! He was always telling her how pretty she was and asking her to do things with him. He even had a pet name for her—Red. And even though she'd been avoiding him lately, he still said hi whenever he saw her at the mall.

Lost in her thoughts, Danielle pushed her tray toward the middle of the table. Since she had dropped him—the last time—Don did seem a tad miffed at her. He might even go out with somebody else, just to make her jealous—which it would! She had to find him—before Ashley or Wendy did—and make it up to him!

But stepping into the mall right after school, Danielle saw that her worst fears were coming true. Ashley and Wendy were hurrying straight for Video Arcade—the exact right place to find Don!

Heading them off in front of Hobart Electronics, Danielle said, "What did you do, cut final period?" They must have, or in her new BMW Danielle would have gotten there ahead of them.

"Worried, Danielle?" Ashley asked, taunting her. Danielle had to admit to herself that Ashley looked fantastic. So did Wendy, for that matter. It was a good thing that Danielle had gone to school in a sensational outfit that day. In her black suede miniskirt and long black silk jacket, she wasn't exactly shabby.

"Worried about what?" she replied casually. "I'm just here to do a little shopping."

"A little shopping?" Wendy laughed, poking Ashley in the side. "Get her! She's not even *thinking* about Don, right?"

"That's right," Danielle told her. "Go ahead and ask him to the dance—both of you. He won't go. Don happens to be a very loyal guy. I haven't had time to ask him yet, but he knows I'm going to. If I were you, I'd get busy lining up your dates. Don's had a thing for me since sixth grade."

"Well, maybe he's grown up a little since then." Ashley sneered. "We're going to find him right now and ask him to the dance."

"Go ahead. I don't care. He's probably at the auto parts store, knowing him—looking for a hand brake or a foot pedal or something—" She chuckled to herself. "That Don, he's got a thing about machines."

"Right. Let's go, Wendy." And with that, the two girls were off, pursuing their quarry.

Danielle watched them go. It was all she could do not to laugh.

And now, to find Don, she thought, heading straight for Video Arcade.

Sure enough, there he was. But he wasn't playing Star Command—he was too busy being congratulated and signing autographs. A crowd of shoppers had surged around him, each trying to shake Don's hand.

"Don!" Danielle called, trying to make herself heard over the well-wishers. "Over here!"

"Red!" he called back, a huge grin spread

across his face. There. He had seen her and was waving back. Soon he had freed himself enough to get over to where she was.

"Think I ought to run for mayor?" he said, joking. He tugged on his old leather jacket, straightening it.

Danielle laughed. That was one of the things she liked best about Don—his sense of humor.

"You are pretty popular," she replied coyly. "Listen, Don, I've got to get to a meeting. I'm on the Sadie Hawkins dance committee, you know, and I was just wondering—"

"Yeeesss?" Don prompted her, smiling as if he knew what she was trying to say.

"Would you like to go with me?" In spite of herself, Danielle bit her lip. If he said no, she'd just have to die.

Don's smile grew broader now and took on a hint of cockiness. "What happened, Red? Suddenly I'm good enough for you? Last few weeks you weren't even talking to me."

"Oh, that—" Danielle tried to stop herself from blushing, but it was impossible. "That was really stupid of me. The pressure from my friends got to me," she admitted.

"I see. But now, since everybody suddenly wants to be seen with me, you do too?"

Danielle's face was so red she could feel her pulse beating in her temples. "D-Don, I've always liked you, you know that," she finally stammered.

Don's dark eyes locked with her emerald ones, and Danielle had to blink back the tears she felt gathering.

"Sadie Hawkins dance, huh?" he said at last. "Why, I suppose I could give it a shot."

"You mean, yes?"

"Yeah, that's what I mean," said Don with a smile. "Red, you got yourself a date."

A surge of warmth went straight through Danielle and for a long time the two of them just stood, gazing at each other, huge smiles ringing their faces.

"Thanks, Don." Laughing with relief, Danielle leaned against his chest, her heart beating at the nearness of him. His strong, muscular arms suddenly wrapped around her, and Danielle sighed, utterly happy. She was going to have what she wanted most in the whole world—the envy of every girl in Merivale—*and* a date with the guy she liked the most in the whole world—Don James!

CHAPTER FOUR

"I'm telling you, Lori, he just doesn't like me anymore!" Patsy Donovan threw herself down on Lori's bed with a moan. "You've got to help me figure out what I'm doing wrong. Whatever it is, I'll fix it!"

Lori finished putting her school books down on her desk and turned around to face her friend with a look of concern. "Patsy, I'm not sure I get this. You say Irv doesn't like you anymore, but didn't you just tell me he walked you home from school today?"

"That doesn't mean anything. He always walks me home on days when we have chem. He's been doing that all year."

"Well, that means something, Patsy!" Lori insisted. "I mean, it's obvious Irv likes you—as a person *and* romantically!"

"Wrong, Lori. He *used* to like me romantically. Last week he stopped." Patsy blew out a

34

big breath and covered her head with a pillow. "Why? Why?" she groaned. "What made him change?"

"Well, on your walk home—was he friendly?" Lori asked with a puzzled look. There had to be some reason that Irv was pulling back from Patsy.

"Yes, he was very friendly. He even held my hand," Patsy answered dolefully, taking the pillow away from her face.

"He held your hand!" cried Lori incredulously. "Patsy, boys don't hold hands with girls they don't like. Especially not boys like Irv. When a boy holds a girl's hand, that's special."

Patsy's hazel eyes brightened for a minute. "That's true," she said, raising herself to her elbows. "And he really held it too. We were joking around and he squeezed it, not hard, just, nice—" Patsy's lips slid into a radiant smile as she thought of Irv, and her eyes took on a glazed, faraway look.

"Patsy, could you be making this whole thing up?" Lori suggested. "When I saw you and Irv after chem class, it seemed to me you guys were fine. Irv's crazy about you. Anybody can see that."

"Really?" Patsy giggled. "Oh, he's so sweet, Lori. He's the sweetest boy I ever met." Patsy's gaze was full of warmth, and there was that smile again. She had it bad for Irv Zalaznick.

Lori couldn't help smiling either. It was so

great that Patsy and Irv had found each other. They both had bloomed in the time they'd been together too. Irv seemed more sure of himself, and so did Patsy. The relationship was obviously a healthy one.

"He wants to take me to a science exhibit at the museum and then to O'Burgers on Saturday night," Patsy added, sighing.

"From chem lab partners to true love," murmured Lori, swept away.

"Arggh!" Patsy's scream wasn't loud, but it was desperate. "Then why has he stopped kissing me? When he left, he said 'Bye, Pats.' He said it real soft, like he does before he's going to kiss me good-by. I sort of sidled up to him so he could reach my face. But he didn't kiss me. He gave my arm one of those little punches again! Does *that* seem like true love to you?"

"Not really." Lori had to admit, a punch on the shoulder wasn't the most romantic way to say good-by to your girlfriend. Lori turned to her mirror and took her barrettes out of her hair. If Nick suddenly stopped kissing her, wouldn't she think there was something seriously wrong between them? Irv's behavior was definitely weird. No wonder Patsy was going out of her mind.

Lori peeked over her image in the mirror and looked at her sad friend. Patsy was on her elbows, lost in thought, her face full of hurt. *If only I could help her.* Lori tried to think of something terribly wise or comforting, but it just didn't come.

Then Patsy tossed her legs over and sat on the edge of the bed. "Okay, Lori," she said, suddenly energized. "I've got a plan. Tell me what you think of this! On Saturday, I borrow my dad's car. I tell Irv *I* want to take *him* out for a change. Then, after the museum, and after O'Burgers, I drive up to Overlook. And when we get there—*I* kiss *him*! Passionately!"

Lori slowly took her hazel-eyed friend in. When Ann had suggested something just like that, Patsy had been mortified. Lori guessed Patsy was now truly desperate—but still, a plan like that just might work.

"Patsy," said Lori like a lieutenant to her troops, "remember, Sadie Hawkins Day is coming up. And even if it wasn't, I still think you should go for it!"

"But what if he doesn't like it?" Patsy asked, suddenly scared.

"He'll like it," said Lori with a laugh. "Don't worry!"

"Rats! Start, darn you!" Lori kicked at the front tire of her trusty old red Spitfire later that night in the mall parking lot. The car was her pride and joy, but just then if it were a living thing, she would have killed it.

It was already quarter to ten. If the car didn't start in one minute, she was going to get home late for her curfew. That meant her parents were likely to ground her. And with the Sadie Hawkins dance and Rob Matthews's party coming up, being grounded was the last thing Lori needed!

"Come on. Be a good little Spitfire—just turn over, that's all I ask." Lori slid behind the wheel and tried the key again. But the engine answered her only with the same strangled chortle.

Ugh. Lori let her head fall to the steering wheel. If only Nick were around! But he'd left the mall hours before to work at his father's warehouse on Route 32. There wasn't any way to reach him there either. Besides, even if she could reach him, she'd still be late getting home. She needed help *now*!

I promise I'll learn about engines. I promise— but please, car, just start now. Lori sighed. Well, this was what she got for being a complete dunce about cars. She'd have to do something about it someday.

Why did males always seem to know about cars? Her father or Nick would have known right away what was wrong with the car. Lori's eyes drifted up over the dashboard to the mall.

Don James! His name popped into her head like a light bulb turning on. Don could fix whatever was wrong with any car. Lori wished it weren't so late. Don would be long gone because the mall was closed up tight.

"Listen," Lori told her car calmly. "I'm going to put the key in your starter. Let me hear that wonderful little purr of yours, and I'll be so happy! Ready? Here we go—" With a grimace, Lori inserted the key and turned it.

Chug. Chug. Chug. There wasn't enough power there to start a lawn mower!

"Rats and double rats!" Lori shouted, slapping the dashboard. Then she got out and gave the tire a good kick. "There! You no-good—"

Sliding back into the car, she leaned against the seat and let out the breath she had been holding. This wasn't the end of the world, she told herself—just the end of freedom as she knew it!

Lori fit her key into the starter once more. This time, lo and behold, the car roared into action! *That last kick must have done the trick!* Lori decided with a laugh. She pulled out of the parking lot and headed for home.

Maybe they won't notice, Lori tried to tell herself. If she didn't run into any traffic or too many lights, she could be home by ten-fifteen. *That's not so bad*, she thought—especially considering that a ten-thirty curfew was much more realistic for a responsible sixteen-year-old. If only her parents would see it that way!

Biting her lip, Lori drove down Main and turned off at Oakwood, and there, she found herself stuck behind a senior citizen—judging by the white hair—who was driving ten miles below the speed limit.

She flicked on the radio to get her mind off the slow journey home. "The time is now ten-fifteen, and all's well in Merivale" came the dee-jay's voice. Lori flicked the dial to shut him up.

Finally she arrived home at ten twenty-five. It could have been worse, she told herself as she hurried out of the car and up the path to the front door. *A lot worse* . . .

Fitting her key in the door, she called out in a voice as bright as she could make it, "Hi, Mom! Hi, Dad! I'm home!" The last thing she wanted to do was make them think she was trying to sneak in unnoticed.

Her parents were in the living room wait-ing for her. Her normally cheerful mother looked tired, and her usually calm father seemed agi-tated. Obviously, Cynthia and George Randall weren't thrilled that she was late.

"Hold on—" Lori began breathlessly. "I can explain."

George Randall stared at her over the top of his reading glasses. Then he folded his paper and put it down on the coffee table in front of him. "Go ahead. I'm listening," he said calmly. "What happened this time? I suppose it was your car?"

Lori looked at her dad in amazement. "You're right! It wouldn't start—that was ex-actly what happened. I left work a little late, went straight to the parking lot, and the car wouldn't start."

"Lori, do you realize that this is the third time you've been late in the past three days?" her mother said.

Lori hung her head and nodded. "I know. And I'm really sorry."

"Why didn't you at least call?" her dad wanted to know. "You know we can't help worrying."

"I would have called," Lori spoke up, "but I wasn't near a phone booth. And besides, I figured I wouldn't be that late."

"I think half an hour is very late, Lori. Especially when you know how your dad and I feel about your curfew."

When she heard that, Lori's blood began to boil. Why was a stupid curfew so important to her parents?

"You know, it's not easy being a parent. You'll find that out someday," murmured her father.

"Well, it isn't easy being a teenager either!" Lori blurted out. "Especially when your parents treat you like you're two years old!"

Lori couldn't believe it. She had always been so close to her mom and dad. They hardly ever fought, and usually her parents were reasonable about most things.

So how come, all of a sudden, they were getting tied in knots over what time she got home at night? True, she had given them an awful fright that time she and Frank O'Conner got stuck in a snowstorm and she had to stay out overnight at Frank's family's cabin. But still, that wasn't her fault! The troopers had told them to turn back because the roads were closed.

"Lori, don't you see? Maybe it's mostly a symbol, but the curfew means a lot to us," her father said.

"But why? You know I can take care of myself. I'm a junior in high school. You know my friends—they're not a bunch of weirdos—so why can't you just trust me? Don't you even believe me about the car?" Lori pleaded, ready to burst into tears.

"Of course I believe you, Lori," her dad said softly. "And we believe *in* you. But it's our job to make the rules. As long as you're living in our house, we're responsible for you."

"Well, can't your rules be a little more realistic? Honestly, a ten o'clock curfew is a little unreasonable. The way it is now, I don't even have time to talk to anybody after work. I always have to rush home. The same goes for weekends. I'm always the first one to leave a party, no matter how much fun I'm having."

Her father looked at her mother. "How much later would you want it to be, Lori?" her mom asked with a sigh.

"Well, an extra half-hour would really help. That would make it ten-thirty on weekdays. And maybe twelve-thirty Friday and Saturday nights. I think that would be a whole lot more realistic."

From the way they were looking at her, Lori could tell they were really thinking about it.

"You know, Lori," said her mother after a while, "I would consider moving your curfew up, but not now, when you've been late three times in a row. If we moved it up now, it would be all wrong."

"I agree," George Randall threw in. "But how about this—if Lori keeps her current curfew for a few more weeks, *then* we'll extend it."

"Sounds good to me," her mother agreed. "But she'll have to keep it religiously, stalled cars or no."

Looking from her father to her mother, Lori could hardly believe her ears. Still, the thought of the dance made her brave enough to ask, "How about if I keep the old curfew for one more week?" If she could get her curfew extended for the Sadie Hawkins dance, and the party afterward, Lori knew she'd be in heaven!

"Okay with me." Her mother nodded. "George?"

Lori's father considered and then agreed. "All right, Lori. Come home on time until a week from Friday night, and on next Saturday, you can stay out till twelve-thirty. But no mistakes till then!"

"Don't worry about it!" Lori said with a relieved laugh. "This is the best news I've had all day. Thanks, you guys!"

"Don't thank us—yet," her dad teased. "Thank us when your curfew is relaxed."

Lori ignored his advice. Planting a kiss on both their cheeks, she hurried to her room. Keeping to her curfew for one more week was going to be no problem—no problem at all!

CHAPTER FIVE

It was late Saturday afternoon, and Danielle was in heaven. Well, really, she was only in O'Burgers, but it *felt* like heaven. There she was, with Don James, man of the hour, basking in the glow of all the attention he was getting. Everyone was sure to be there soon—Ashley Shepard, Wendy Carter, Jane Haggerty, and a bunch of other Atwood girls.

"Oh! Look! There's Danielle!" Danielle craned her neck, and sure enough, there was Ashley making her way to the table where Danielle and Don were sitting. Behind Ashley were Wendy Carter, wearing a new black leather jacket, and Jane Haggerty in a pair of acid-washed blue jeans. Suddenly Don James–style clothes were the rage of Atwood aristocracy.

"Hi, Danielle!" Ashley said her hello as if she was surprised to see Danielle, which she wasn't, Danielle knew. Danielle had practically broadcast the fact that she and Don would be at O'Burgers. After all, she didn't want it to go unnoticed that she and Don were an item—even if it was too soon to call it that. More than that, she wanted any potential rivals to get the message loud and clear—*no trespassing*.

"Hello, Ashley," cooed Danielle with just a hint of triumph exuding from her emerald eyes.

Ashley ignored Danielle completely. "Hi, Don," she purred, her eyes riveted on his handsome face and shiny black hair.

"Um, oh, hi." Don looked confused. He squinted his dark Gypsy eyes and took Ashley in with a puzzled look. "Are you a friend of Danielle's?" he finally blurted out.

To that, Ashley responded with a giggle—as if Don were the wittiest guy in the entire universe.

"Oh, Danielle, I was wondering about that French assignment—" Jane Haggerty's eyes were fixed on Don as she made her way up to their table.

"We didn't have any French assignment this week, Jane," Danielle replied.

"Oh. And you're Don James, aren't you?" Jane said it as if she were saying, And you just won an Academy Award, didn't you?

Don looked Jane over from head to toe. "Yeah, I'm Don. And you're—?"

Jane was horrified that she wasn't known,

but she quickly recovered and broke out in her version of a charming smile. "I'm the managing editor of the Atwood *Tattler*. Maybe you'd like to give me an interview?"

"Maybe," said Don with a noncommittal shrug. "But I wouldn't hold my breath."

Danielle had to bite her lip to keep from laughing. The last time she had been out with Don, Jane Haggerty had made her life miserable. Jane had acted as if Danielle were slumming with Don. Now Jane was getting hers. Don seemed to sense a natural enemy when he saw one.

"Ahem! Don and I really don't have much time—if you don't mind," said Danielle sweetly, to break up the group of Atwood girls that was standing beside their table openly ogling Don.

"Sure, Danielle," purred Ashley. "Oh, and nice to see you, Don—" Ashley's eyes were practically glued to his face now. Wendy had to poke her in the ribs to get her to move away from Danielle's table.

"Now I know why movie stars are always complaining they want their privacy," said Don, reaching for his water. "I thought it was just going to be me and you, not Grand Central Station, you know?"

"Can I help it if everybody wants to get a look at you?" Danielle asked innocently.

"Can I help it if it makes me uncomfortable?" Don said, and grinned slowly until the smile lit up his smoldering dark eyes. Sliding his arm along the tabletop, he reached out and encircled her hand. "Listen, why don't we get a table in the back?" he said conspiratorially. "It'll be more private."

"I've got an even better idea. Let's get out of here!" she said, suddenly standing up and holding his hand.

"Where we going?" Don asked.

"You'll find out," Danielle said, motioning to the confused waitress that they weren't going to stay. She pulled Don out onto the promenade.

"Okay, Red. You lead. I'll follow." Don chuckled. With a giggle, Danielle slipped her arm around his waist, hooking her thumb into one of his belt loops. They made their way down the mall, laughing. One of the greatest things about being with Don was the incredible sense of fun he brought wherever he went. Even just walking down the mall with him seemed like an adventure, and he brought that sense of adventure out in Danielle too. With him, she felt like a free spirit.

Suddenly Danielle pulled him from the center of the mall to a door that led to a seldom-used staircase. "Here we can have some privacy," she teased, opening the door.

"Well, pretty neat," said Don when the

stairway door closed behind them. "We're all alone—except for mall security, of course." Don pointed up to a camera mounted on the wall. "Hi, Archie. Hi, Vince." He waved. "As you can see, I'm in the stairwell, and I'm going to kiss this girl here, right now, so please close your eyes for a minute." With a wicked grin Don slipped his arms around Danielle, pulling her close. Leisurely he bent his head and gently placed his warm lips against hers.

Danielle felt as though her heart were pumping pure liquid gold. Don was so tender, yet so incredibly exciting. He was so cool too—so different, so unique—and his kiss was pure fire.

When it was over, he leaned back and grinned at her. Gently taking her arm, he asked, "So, Red—where to?"

"I have two places in mind—" Danielle replied, still a little breathless. "First, I thought I'd introduce you to my favorite indoor sport—shopping." Being with Don in public was wonderful, but the way he dressed could definitely stand some improvement. The first stop Danielle had in mind was Men in Motion, the clothing store right next to Facades.

Don looked confused, but Danielle just grabbed him by the hand and guided him to the escalator and up three flights to the privileged world on the fourth level. "This is going to be *fantastic!*" she gushed.

"If there's another group of sightseers where

we're going, just forget it," said Don with a slight frown lining his forehead.

"Don't worry. Nobody is going to look for *you* where *we're* going." Danielle laughed. It was true. Don had probably never been inside Men in Motion.

"Look, I was thinking, let's just go hang out—the duck pond or something," said Don uncomfortably when they stepped onto the fourth floor. "Shopping isn't exactly my—"

"Come on," she said, tugging on the sleeve of his black leather jacket and dragging him across to the store.

"Are we just window-shopping, or do you have something more ambitious in mind?" Don wanted to know.

"Window-shop? No, no, you need a suit!"

"What for? I promise I'll rent a tux for Sadie Hawkins—" Don protested.

Danielle interrupted. "Don James! You're an important person in this town! You're going to be getting an award from the mayor tomorrow and meeting all kinds of influential people—starting tonight—with my parents!"

"Meet your parents?" In all the time she'd known him, Danielle had never seen Don at a loss for words.

"And I can't very well introduce you to them looking like *that*." She glanced at the hole in the knee of his jeans, and his dull leather jacket.

But Don just continued to look at her as if she were from Mars. "Your *parents*?" he finally spit out.

Danielle's green eyes twinkled mischievously. When the girls heard she'd brought Don home to meet her folks, they'd die, absolutely *die*!

Of course she wouldn't tell her parents where he worked—nothing personal about him. She'd just say he was a new kid at Atwood—she'd think of something, she knew.

Or maybe she wouldn't lie about him. After all, Don was a hero. Her parents knew all about his daring rescue. For once, her snobby mother would have to be proud of her.

"I don't get it," said Don with a shake of his head. "Two days ago you were avoiding me. Now you're bringing me home to meet the folks. That's a pretty sudden change of heart, Red."

Danielle couldn't help blushing. Sure, the fact that Don was a hero did make bringing him home a lot easier. But still, she had liked him long before Baby Eddie came into the picture. "Don," she said, looking up at him. "I've always been proud of who you are. You know that."

"Then how come I've got to show up in a suit? Why can't I just come as I am?"

"Look"—Danielle frowned—"when you invite me to dinner at your place, I'll distress a pair of my Calvins and show up with broken nails, okay?"

Don seemed to get the point. "I guess it won't hurt to check out some stuff."

Danielle shot Don a sly smile. "When you see how fantastic you look in a suit, you'll want to wear one all the time," she said.

Don threw his head back and laughed out loud. "Maybe, Red. I guess with a girl like you around, anything's possible."

Their arms around each other's waists, Danielle and Don were still smiling as they strolled through the open doorway into Men in Motion.

"Hi," Danielle said to the salesman who stood by the three-way mirror. "We'd like to look at suits. My friend here has got an award ceremony coming up—you know, the baby, the catch—"

The salesman's face brightened suddenly. "Of course!" he said. "You're Don James! I'm very honored to meet you!"

Don winced as the man patted him on the shoulder that was still sore.

"You know, it's people like you who make our society great," the salesman was saying enthusiastically.

While Don stood there, looking lost, Danielle began pushing through the racks. *Gray—Don in gray. It's brilliant!* He'd look absolutely presidential! A subtle gray would make his dark, rugged looks really stand out.

And half an hour later, when Don stood in front of the mirror wearing a gray suit, white-on-white shirt, and dark blue print tie, Danielle had no doubt about it. It wasn't that he looked bad in leather and denim—he couldn't look bad in anything—but Don James was *born* to wear suits. Except for his hair, which needed a trim and styling, and his hands, which were in dire need of a manicure, Don could have been a top model.

"Turn around again," said Danielle appreciatively. Then, "You look fantastic!"

Don regarded his image with an uncomfortable shrug. "Is this wool or something?" he asked, squirming inside the suit. "It itches."

"Don—it's fabulous!" Danielle gushed. "Buy it."

"I don't know, Red—" Danielle could tell Don was calculating the cost. "After I get the award money it's no problem. But right now—"

"No problem! I'll put it on my plastic," said Danielle. "You can pay me back."

"Plus interest," Don said with a meaningful look. Danielle knew Don was proud about money. He didn't have a lot of it, but he always paid his own way. That was something else Danielle really liked about him.

"Okay," he called to the salesman standing

behind the counter. "Wrap up my other stuff. I'll wear this out of the store."

Don looked nervous while he waited for Danielle to make the transaction. "I hope I don't regret this," he murmured half to himself.

"You won't," said Danielle, throwing him a thousand-watt smile. "Trust me."

Don raised one eyebrow and lowered his chin in a way that made her smile. "Trust you, huh?" he teased. "I don't know about this, Red."

Stepping out onto the promenade, Danielle slid her hand along the soft woolen fabric of Don's new jacket. It felt fantastic. Danielle gazed up at him with a warm smile, and he shook his head, amused. "This really turns you on, doesn't it?" he asked, beaming.

"Danielle!" That voice could belong to only one person—Teresa Woods. There she was, coming up the opposite side of the escalator as they traveled down. And from the look on Teresa's face, Danielle could tell she was mightily impressed.

Not only had Danielle bagged Don James, but she had transformed him into absolute perfection—and all in one day!

CHAPTER SIX

"This thing handles pretty well." Don ran his hands over the steering wheel of Danielle's gleaming white BMW with a smile. "But I still like my T-bird."

"Make a right here," she said, ignoring that last remark. There was no way she could show up at her house in an old beat-up car. Having Don drive them in her car made a lot more sense.

"We're the third gate on the right," she told him when they turned into Wood Hollow Hills. The homes were all modern mansions set far back from the road. Danielle's father had designed them all to blend in with the heavily wooded landscape. And naturally, he had designed the best for himself.

"This gate?" he asked, pulling under a wrought-iron sign that arched high above them. "Guess it is," he said, turning around to read THE SHARPS.

"You got it." Danielle laughed and glanced sideways at him. Soon, through the bare branches of the trees lining the drive, the house came into view.

"Whew." Don whistled, taking it all in. "Not exactly a shack."

Almost anybody would've been impressed by the Sharp home. It was three stories of wood and glass, with floodlights, skylights, and decks surrounding much of it. A gardener had finished pruning and was now wheeling a cart full of branches back to the wooded area of the estate.

"That your father?" asked Don when they got out of the car.

Danielle looked over at the gardener with his baggy work pants and let out a giggle. "No, that's our gardener."

"Hi, how you doing?" Don called as they strode up to the front door. The gardener nodded and watched Danielle and Don go to the door.

After taking out her key, Danielle fitted it into the huge carved oak door. "Hi," she called out cheerfully to anybody who was there.

The maid peeked into the entryway. "Hello, Miss Sharp. Your mother is upstairs, and your dad is in his study," she said, ignoring Don completely.

"Thanks, Grace," Danielle replied. Then she turned to Don. "Let's get a soda."

The walk to the kitchen was long, taking them past the living room and dining room. Don looked at the paintings and prints, taking in every detail of the house as if he were going to be quizzed on them.

Danielle poked her head into her father's study. Inside, Mike Sharp was standing at his desk, which was covered with blueprints. A look of concentration was on his face, but when he looked up and noticed Danielle, he broke into a grin. "Hi, honey."

Danielle stepped back and pulled Don into her father's view.

"Hi, Dad. I brought someone for dinner. Dad, this is Don James. Don, my father." Danielle looked from one man to the other with a huge grin on her face. Lately, her wildest fantasies seemed to be coming true!

"Don James? Why, you're the kid who saved that baby!" said Mr. Sharp, clasping Don's hand in his.

Don nodded modestly and returned Mike Sharp's handshake. "Glad to meet you, sir."

"That was some feat," her father said, patting Don on the back. "Congratulations."

Casting a fond look at Don, Danielle took his arm and pulled him gently toward the kitchen. "We're going to get a soda," she explained. "See you later, Daddy."

As they walked away, Danielle could tell that her father was impressed. And why not?

Don was not only a hero, but in his new suit he looked as if he were worth about a jillion dollars.

In the kitchen Don ran his hand through his hair in mock relief. "Whoa, Red. This is intense," he said.

Danielle's green eyes widened. "You mean being here, meeting my parents?"

"No wonder you walk around acting like a princess. This place is a palace."

"We like it," said Danielle with a smile. "Now, what would you like? Mineral water? Coke? Ginger ale?"

"I'll try some of that stuff," said Don, pointing to the Perrier.

"I just ordered fifty cases of it for the Sadie Hawkins dance. It's going to be so great! We're going to have tropical punch, Perrier, and a whole assortment of old-fashioned sodas—cream, root beer, even sarsaparilla. Isn't that neat? It was my idea, actually." Danielle leaned against the central cooking island and took in Don. He *was* fun to be with.

"Am I going to pick you up on my bike?" Don asked, his eyes sparkling mischievously.

Danielle's eyes opened wide and she looked panicked for an instant. "Are you kidding? No way! I'll be wearing a formal gown! Besides, I have to get there early to set up. I'll meet you there."

"Great." Don took the drink she was offering and leaned back on his elbows next to her against the island. They didn't say anything but just stared into each other's eyes. The smiles they were wearing were warmer than the Caribbean sun at noon.

Just then the door of the kitchen swung open and in walked Serena Sharp. As always, Danielle's mother looked fabulous. In fact, Danielle couldn't remember the last time she'd seen her mom without makeup. That day she wore black silk pants, a white silk shirt, and a wide band of gold around her neck. For Serena Sharp, it was a casual outfit, perfect for an evening at home.

"Hi, Mom," Danielle said with a smile.

"Danielle! Hello—and hello," she said pleasantly, looking straight at Don.

Good old Serena, thought Danielle about her mother. *Grace under fire.* Danielle's mom appeared totally calm and unflustered, as if Danielle brought strange guys into the kitchen every night.

"Mom, I'd like you to meet Don James. Don, this is my mother." Danielle made the introduction just the way her mother had taught her to make it.

"Hello, Don, nice to meet you," said her mother warmly, and this time Danielle thought the friendliness seemed genuine. Danielle was surprised. Obviously, Serena was in a good mood. Her parents had probably made up from the screaming fight they'd had last night.

"Hi, Mrs. Sharp," said Don simply.

"Mom, can Don stay for dinner?" asked Danielle, throwing her mother one of her little-girl smiles and pouring herself some more soda.

Her mother's eyes widened in surprise, but she answered, "Of course, darling. He'd be very welcome."

Don smiled uncomfortably. "Thank you, Mrs. Sharp. This is certainly a very nice home," he said, reaching for the soda and gulping some down.

"Thank you, Don. It'll look a lot better when I get the new vertical blinds installed, but for now it'll just have to do."

So, they had made up. One of the things about her mom that drove her dad crazy was that Serena was never satisfied with things as they were. She'd ordered new drapes just a few weeks earlier, but now she insisted that she had to have vertical blinds. That was what the big fight had been about, and obviously Serena had won.

"Are you a classmate of Danielle's?" her mother asked pleasantly.

Danielle was just about to interrupt when a horn beeped in the side driveway. Outside the window was the blue and gold van from Premier Caterers, the people who supplied most of the Sharps' meals.

"Oh! Excuse me, please. Grace!" Danielle's mother called to the maid, who was setting the dining room table. "Premier is here. Also, please set another place and order another dinner. Danielle's friend will be joining us. Well," she said, turning back to Danielle and Don, "let's move to the living room. We'll be more comfortable there."

Following Mrs. Sharp, Don shot Danielle a look that seemed to say How am I doing? Danielle grinned and flashed him a dazzling smile that said Keep it up!

"Wait a minute," said Mrs. Sharp when they got to the immense modern living room. "Aren't you the boy who saved that little baby?" Serena's face had just twisted into a sneer. Danielle knew her mother well enough to guess exactly what she was thinking. The newspaper write-up about Don mentioned that he was a Merivale High student who worked part-time as an auto mechanic.

Horrified, Danielle jumped up. "Oh! Mom!" she cried. "I just remembered! I need to talk to you, in private—it's about something that happened in school. Sorry, Don. We'll be right back."

Danielle stood up. It wasn't the best lie she'd ever come up with, but it worked.

"Please excuse us a moment," her mother told Don before she followed Danielle into the dining room.

As soon as they were alone, Danielle closed the door. "It's not really about school, Mom.

It's about Don." Danielle could see her mother's face tighten. "He's not really who he says he is."

That statement certainly aroused her mother's curiosity. "What are you talking about, Danielle!"

"Well, you know how in the paper and on the news they were saying Don had a job in a gas station and all—"

"Yes . . . ?"

"Well, that part is true. But see, Don's an orphan—" Danielle was trying to get her brain to work fast, but she had to collect her thoughts to make the lie seem real.

"An orphan? Really?"

"Mom," Danielle began again. "You know, the James family from Boston—"

"No, I don't believe I've ever heard of them—"

"Well, you know Henry James and William James. Anyway, Don's from that line. But his parents were killed in a polo meet in Brazil while he was still a baby, and he's just moved to Merivale. I guess he feels very shy. I guess he doesn't know who really likes him and who's just after all the money he inherited. It's not easy to be seventeen years old and have fifty million dollars in trust for you."

"Oh, dear," said Serena, surprised. "I guess not—"

"Anyway, that's why he took the job at the

gas station. He's trying to pretend he's just like everybody else, and he'd be really upset if he knew I told you the truth. So please, don't ask him any more questions about himself, okay?"

Her mother's face softened into a smile, and she took her daughter by the arm. "Danielle dear, I'm really impressed by your understanding. And I promise, I won't ask your friend any personal questions. But I must say, he *is* awfully good-looking. And fifty million dollars, well—that's a lot of money."

"I know," said Danielle, relieved to be telling the truth. "Well, we'd better go back— Oh, Mom, I haven't told Daddy about this. Don would die if he thought everyone knew. So please just go along with whatever is said. Okay?"

Since she was a little girl, Danielle's parents had always loved to be set against each other. This time was no exception.

"Don't worry, darling. I won't say a word."

Danielle's father must have joined Don in the living room while Danielle and her mother were gone. When the women got back the men were deep in conversation.

"Maybe you'll take a look under the hood sometime, Don," her dad was saying. "I'd appreciate it, I can tell you. I haven't spoken to anyone who knew what they were talking about since I got the stupid thing."

"What's that, darling?" asked Mrs. Sharp, joining the conversation.

"Oh, that old MG I bought. Don here tells me the whole problem with it could be the crankshaft. Wouldn't that be a kick in the head? I must've spent two thousand bucks trying to get that thing together—"

"It's his hobby," Serena explained to Don. "My husband loves to spend money on broken-down cars—"

"Now, an MG four-sixty is hardly a broken-down car, Serena," Danielle's dad countered. "She doesn't understand how a car can get to you," he told Don.

"Well, I don't suppose a few thousand dollars would mean much to you," Mrs. Sharp said to Don, "but—"

"Mom!" chided Danielle, throwing her mother a look.

"Oh, excuse me." Mrs. Sharp blushed. "Now, shall we go to the table? I think Grace has everything ready."

The table was set with gold-edged dinner plates, silver flatware, and delicate crystal glasses.

"Don, you sit here," Mrs. Sharp commanded pleasantly. "And Danielle is here."

Don immediately went to Danielle's chair and held it for her. He was acting as if he went to fancy dinners every night of the week. Danielle was amazed, and pleased.

As her mom consulted with Grace and her dad went to answer the phone, Danielle smiled and whispered, "Not bad, Don."

Don replied with a half wink that almost made her swoon. "I told you, you under-estimate me, Red. You always have."

"So, what's on the menu tonight, Serena?" asked Mike Sharp with a ceremonious wink as he returned to his place. "Mrs. Sharp is a pre-miére cook." Only the gleam of mischief in his eye gave him away.

"Stop, you," Danielle's mother teased back as Grace served them each a portion of steam-ing duckling and orange sauce. "Don knows perfectly well this dinner came from the cater-ers, don't you, Don?"

"Well, wherever it came from, it sure looks good," Don replied with a grin. "I love chicken."

"It's duckling. Strictly speaking, that is," said Mrs. Sharp with an amused smile. It was amazing how relaxed her mother could be when things were going well for her, Danielle thought. And thinking she was in the presence of major money just added to Serena's charm.

"Well, if you ask me, the only way to eat these things is with your fingers," Danielle's father mumbled, snapping a leg off in his hand. Her father had a thing about "celebrating his working-class roots"—as her mother put it.

For one panicky moment Danielle was afraid Don would do the same thing. But he didn't. Instead, he leaned forward and said, "You know, Mr. Sharp, I really admire the way you've done all this on your own. I hope I'll be able to say the same about myself someday." And, having thrown a compliment her father's way, Don proceeded to cut up his duckling delicately with his knife and fork, with a nod to Mrs. Sharp. In one deft maneuver he had succeeded in winning over both her parents!

Danielle glanced at her watch as she finished up her dessert. Nine o'clock. The evening was marching on, and she didn't want to spend it all at home with her parents. No, she had other plans for Don James that night.

"Oops! Mom, Dad, I forgot to tell you, Don and I have to be someplace." She glanced at her diamond-studded gold watch again. "There's a party at Ben Frye's place."

"Oh?" Her mother seemed surprised, and no wonder. Danielle had never mentioned anything about any party because she'd just made it up.

"Well, I hope you'll bring Don back again soon," she said sincerely, giving Don a warm smile and a pat on the hand.

"Right," echoed her dad. "And next time we can get under the hood together. So come in work clothes—old jeans or something."

"Yes, sir." Don nodded.

"Well, shall we go?" asked Danielle, standing up. "We'll be late if we don't hurry. Bye, Mom. Bye, Dad!"

"Take care, Mrs. Sharp, Mr. Sharp. See you again. And thanks for a terrific dinner."

Soon Danielle and Don were out the door and in her car.

"Your folks are all right, you know?" said Don as Danielle inserted the key.

Danielle snorted. "They're okay, I guess," she admitted. "But they fight all the time. It drives me crazy."

"Well, anytime you want to trade—" Don offered with a smile. "So, can I take this tie off now? My neck is starting to break out in a rash."

"Be my guest," said Danielle, turning off the main road and steering the car up a hill.

"Wrong way, Red."

"Don't worry," Danielle replied, a twinkle in her eye. "We're not going to Ben's. I have something else in mind."

A minute later the answer was obvious. The car turned onto Overlook Terrace. "I see." He grinned and leaned back against the soft leather car seat, putting his hands behind his head, elbows to the sides. "Well, well, well."

Wearing a sly smile, Danielle pulled her BMW into the scenic view parking lot at the side of the road. Nearby were a dozen or so other cars, some with motors idling to keep the occupants warm on the cold night. Danielle and Don were at Merivale's favorite parking spot.

Danielle put the car in park and turned to Don. "Now do you understand why I wanted to get out of there?" she purred.

"I'm beginning to," he said with a grin, sliding his left arm along the top of Danielle's seat.

"Well, let me explain it a little better," she whispered, running her hands through his hair. And before he could say a word, she silenced him with a sizzling kiss.

CHAPTER SEVEN

"Mmmmm—"

Lori Randall gazed into Nick's sparkling aquamarine eyes and sighed. He had to be the world's greatest kisser. Wiping off the windshield with the sleeve of her coat, she looked out at the twinkling lights of Merivale far below them. If this wasn't heaven, it was definitely the next best thing.

"Oh, Nick," she whispered, settling back into his arms, "we're so lucky, aren't we?"

"Mmmm—" Nick agreed with a sigh. "Oh, Lori, Lori—" Running his hands through her soft golden hair, he drew her to him for another kiss. One more kiss and Lori knew she'd forget where she was completely.

"Um, Nick, I hate to say this," she murmured, stroking his cheek tenderly. "But I have my curfew to think about. Just one more week. If I'm going to go to Rob Matthews's party after the Sadie Hawkins dance, I'd better get home soon."

Nick's warm, contented smile slid into a disappointed frown. He pushed back the sleeve of his coat and looked at his watch. "Uh-oh. Would you believe it's a quarter to twelve already?" he said with a wince.

"Uh-oh is right." That left only fifteen minutes to get back. "We'd better leave—now," she said hurriedly. Then, "Thank goodness it's only for one more week. I can't wait to get this curfew rolled back!"

"Me neither," Nick said with a grin. "But for tonight, here goes. Don't worry, Cynthia and George, she's on her way." Nick reached for the key and turned it in the ignition.

Grrr—rrrrr—rrrrr— The Camaro sounded sick.

"Oh, no," moaned Lori, covering her face with her hands. "I don't believe this."

"Well, let's not despair." Nick let go of the key. "It probably just needs to warm up. Let me try again."

Grrrrrrrrrr—rrrrrrr . . . The engine was making a different sound from the one her Spitfire had made a few nights before, but it sounded just as sick.

"Nick," said Lori, the fear rising in her voice. "You didn't flood the engine, did you?"

"I don't think so," Nick said, trying again

with the same results. "I'd better get out and look under the hood."

"All right, but hurry—please. I can't afford to blow it tonight." Lori shivered. All the warmth she and Nick had generated inside the car disappeared the instant he opened the door. Lori bundled herself up inside her down coat as Nick disappeared behind the hood. If she didn't get home on time tonight, her curfew might *never* be rolled back!

A moment later Nick was back inside the car, blowing on his hands. He didn't look exactly optimistic. "It's hard to see," he said, trying the engine again without success.

"You don't have a flashlight?" asked Lori helplessly.

"Nope."

"What are we going to do now?" she asked impatiently. "I've got to be home in ten minutes."

"I know," he replied. "I hate to say this, Lori, but I think we're going to have to get some help."

"Some help?" she repeated, her voice weakening. "Do you know how long it'll take to get a tow truck up here?"

"No, I mean, we could see if anybody else up here knows anything about cars, or at least has a flashlight."

Lori sat there for a moment, stunned. "You mean, knock on car doors?" she whispered.

Interrupting anyone at Overlook Drive was totally embarrassing.

"That's exactly what I mean."

"But—but we can't do that. People come up here to—be together."

"I know. But what choice do we have?"

Nick was right. "Okay," Lori said with as much of a smile as she could muster.

"I'll start at one end of the line. You take the other. Maybe we'll get lucky quick," said Nick, reaching for the car door.

Gritting her teeth, Lori opened her door and headed for the car to the far left of her.

As the frosted window rolled down, Lori nearly sank into her shoes.

"What do you think you're doing?" came an angry voice. Lori recognized Gina Nichols right away. Gina was Merivale High's head cheerleader, and Lori's worst enemy. And next to Gina—instead of her boyfriend, Jack Baxter—was Atwood's Greg Gilbert!

Lori felt herself blush down through the roots of her hair. Gina and Jack, Merivale's quarterback, had been an item all year long—and here was Gina, parked up at the Overlook with Greg, an Atwood guy who'd been dating Georgia Ross ever since junior high!

"Lori Randall, you've certainly got your nerve!" hissed Gina, wild-eyed. Her hair was a total mess, and Greg, all rumpled, didn't look much better. "If you breathe a word of this to anyone—" Gina sputtered as Greg turned away.

"Oh, no! Don't worry, Gina, I won't say anything," Lori whispered. "It's just that Nick's car won't start, and I—"

"Well, that's just too bad for you!" Gina shot back. "I wouldn't help you if you were stuck on top of an iceberg at the North Pole!" And with that, she rolled up the window and locked the car door.

Feeling like a total jerk, Lori went on to the next car and tapped on the window. This time, it was Patsy Donovan's face that greeted hers.

"Lori!" cried Patsy. "Um—hi!" Seated next to Patsy was a flustered Irv Zalaznick, with lipstick smears on his cheeks and mouth.

"Hi, you two. Sorry to interrupt. It's just that Nick's car won't start, and—oh, never mind," she sputtered, feeling like a complete fool.

"I don't know much about cars, but maybe I can help," said Irv, getting out of Patsy's father's car. "Where is it?"

"Over there," Lori pointed to Nick's Camaro. "Thanks, Irv." Then she let her voice fall to a whisper. "How's it going in there?" she asked.

"Well, I thought I was getting somewhere for a minute. You've got a lousy sense of timing, Lori," Patsy complained good-naturedly.

"Sorry," Lori said sincerely. " Well, I'd better try another car."

"Let me know if I can help," Patsy offered.

"Thanks, Pats." Lori took a breath and tried the next car. From inside the fogged-up windows the face of Jane Haggerty was beginning to come into view. Beside her sat—*no*! It was unbelievable. And yet, there he was—Keith Canfield, Atwood's resident insect freak, the boy Danielle had had such a crush on.

"Do you know anything about cars?" Lori asked through the window, her teeth chattering from the cold.

"No! And neither does Keith!" said an embarrassed Jane, turning her back to Lori.

Looking back at Nick's car, Lori saw Nick and Irv standing in front of the hood. "Any luck?" she called from where she was.

"No!" Nick shouted back. "Keep trying!"

Just as he said it, Lori noticed the white BMW. Danielle! If rumor had it right, the boy beside her cousin would be Don James!

Tap, tap, tap—

With a toss of her fiery hair, Danielle gazed through the car window. Beside her was Don James—who was wearing a suit, of all things!

"Lori?" Danielle said, a puzzled look on her face. "What are you doing here?"

"Same as you, I imagine," Lori answered with a shy grin. "But Nick's car won't start. I'm hoping Don can help."

"Sorry, we're kind of involved—" Danielle

started to say. But before she could finish, Don was out of the car.

"Where you parked, Lori?" he asked as Danielle stared at them, annoyed.

"Right over there." Lori pointed. "Nick!" she called out as they went. "I found Don James!"

Don and Lori began making their way to Nick, trailed by a simmering Danielle.

"Great," said Nick as they reached his car. "I can't figure it out, Don. It's not flooded or anything, and the battery's pretty new— Thing is, I haven't got a flashlight."

"Okay," said Don, peering under the hood. "You've got to *feel* these things anyway." He removed his suit jacket and thrust it at Danielle. "Hold this, will you?" he instructed with the concentration of a surgeon about to operate.

Bending under the hood, as Lori, Irv, Nick, and Danielle looked on, Don let out a whistle. "I think I found your problem. Let's see . . ." With that, he twisted a few wires, then said, "Try it now."

Nick hopped into the driver's seat and turned the key in the ignition. The car started up at once, the engine purring like a kitten.

"There you go." Don smiled, wiping his hands on a tissue that Danielle handed him.

"Thanks a million, Don," said Lori, beaming. "I don't know what we would have done without you."

"Anytime," Don replied. Then, turning to Danielle, "Well, shall we get back to—you know—" Even in the dark, Lori could see her cousin's blush.

"Okay, Lori," said a flustered Danielle. "I guess Don took care of the problem for you."

"Thanks, Don. Thanks, Irv. And of course, thank you, Dani," said Lori, piling into Nick's car and shutting the door behind her. "Whew!" she said with a smile. "What time is it now?"

"Just about twelve," answered Nick, leaning over to give her one last kiss. "I'll have you home by a quarter after."

"Thanks, Nick," said Lori as cheerfully as she could manage. How could she tell him that a quarter after wasn't going to be good enough? When Lori's parents caught her walking in after her curfew *again*, it would be all over.

CHAPTER EIGHT

Lori threw open the front door as Nick's Camaro peeled out of the driveway. "Mom? Dad? I'm home!" she said, looking around the living room. The floor lamp behind the blue print love seat was on, but there was no sign of her parents.

"Hello?" she called again—this time into the kitchen. No answer.

Maybe they were in bed. Bounding across the living room, she looked into their room to see if the lights were on. But just then, Trish Van Horne, Mark and Teddy's babysitter, whose mother worked with Lori's mother, appeared at Mark's room.

"Hi, Lori," Trish whispered cheerfully, following Lori to the living room. "Would you believe Mark just fell asleep now? He made me read his story at least six hundred times! Teddy conked out at nine." Trish fell into the love seat in a gesture of mock exhaustion. Then, with a laugh, she sat up. "They have energy, Lori, I'll tell you that!"

Lori laughed. As their bigger sister, she knew all about that. "Do you know where my parents are?" she asked, taking her coat off and hanging it in the hall closet.

"Yes, they called. They were having such a good time they decided to stay longer. They said they'd be here by midnight."

"Right! Tonight's their bridge game. Oh, thank goodness!" This time it was Lori who collapsed onto the sofa in sheer relief. "Whew, that was a close one. Thank you, universe!" She clapped her hands happily.

"Lori—?" Trish asked with a puzzled look.

"Curfew trouble," Lori explained with a frown. "I was supposed to be home by the stroke of midnight or turn into a pumpkin."

"Well, it's only twelve-thirty," said Trish, glancing at her watch with an understanding shrug.

"I wish my parents could see it like that, Trish. They have a thing about my curfew. To them it's some kind of symbol of my entire character, or a test of obedience or something. They're really strict about it," Lori told her. "This past week we had a big fight and they finally said they'd make it ten-thirty on week-days and twelve-thirty on weekends—*if* I got home on time until next Saturday. I really thought I blew it tonight."

"My curfew is twelve-thirty on weekends," said Trish, who was only fifteen.

"See? I kept telling them twelve was too early for a person my age!" said Lori. "It's really ridiculous! And next weekend is the Sadie Hawkins dance at Atwood and a party after, so I really want it changed by then."

Lori kicked off her shoes and tucked her ankles up under her knees. The fact was, she felt just a little annoyed at her mom and dad for putting her through all this.

Just then, laughter on the other side of the front door signaled that George and Cynthia Randall were home. George Randall pushed open the door, and her mother stepped into the room with a radiant smile. Obviously, they had had a great time.

"Hi, Lori," her dad said with a happy grin. "Hi, Trish."

"Dad! Mom!" Lori looked jokingly at her bare wrist and shook a finger at her folks. "Hey! You're late! You said you'd be home by midnight!"

Her parents laughed good-naturedly. Her mother took off her coat while Trish got hers on.

"I can walk home, Mr. Randall," said Trish. "You don't have to drive me. It's not that far."

"That's okay, Trish. I'd rather play it safe," said Mr. Randall.

Lori's mother took Lori in with a serious look. "Okay, Lori. I can't resist asking. What time did *you* get in?"

Lori's face turned bright red as she groped for the right way to put it. It was going to be hard telling them that Nick's car had had a problem, and yet, that was the truth!

But Trish broke the silence. "I remember because I'd just gotten Mark down. It was ten of twelve," she said, coming to the rescue.

"Good, Lori," said her mother. "Way to go!"

Lori shrugged casually. "Well, you know, I really wanted to get here on time tonight," she said truthfully but with an uncomfortable gulp. Lying to her parents wasn't exactly her style, but she wasn't going to say Trish was wrong. Not when everything was riding on her being on time.

"Bye, Lori," said Trish at the door with a sneaky little smile.

"So long, Trish. And thanks—for baby-sitting, that is. Good night, Mom." Lori said, bounding for her room. The quicker she got out of there the better she'd feel!

"Well, Red, I guess this is where I get off—"

Danielle cut the motor in the mall parking lot and turned to Don. "Will I see you tomorrow?" she asked, looking longingly into his smoky dark eyes.

"Sure, why not? I'm due at the mall at three to accept that award and all. Want to meet me there? We can go out after or something," he suggested, running a finger through her lustrous hair.

"That'll be fun— Well, bye for now, I guess—"

"Mmmm—" he replied, drawing her to him for a last, lingering kiss.

Danielle shivered with delight. Of all the boys she'd ever gone out with, Don was definitely the greatest. Everything about him was so unique— the way he looked at life, the things he said, and even the delicious scent of him. He made her feel so relaxed, and so open. Danielle really liked who she was around him too. And now *he* was a real somebody around town. From now on, they'd be inseparable—the hottest couple in Merivale!

Reaching into the back seat and carefully picking up his new suit jacket, Don tossed her a wink. "Well, till tomorrow, Red," he said, opening the door and getting out. Danielle blew a kiss and watched him take off across the deserted parking lot.

Don's bike was in the underground parking lot, so he took the short cut through the loading area.

Walking up to the mall, he turned around once more and watched Danielle still looking at him. He waved, and she gave her horn a little beep to say good-by.

With a smile that wouldn't quit, Don watched the BMW head out of the lot. Life had never been sweeter.

What a turnabout! thought Don. Just a week before he couldn't get anywhere with Danielle and now she wanted to see him all the time. *Thank you, Baby Eddie*, Don laughed to himself.

Suddenly Don James had become the big hero in Merivale. Suddenly everybody wanted to get close to him—especially girls! Everywhere he went they were ogling him, calling out his name, and giggling. It felt great, but the best part was that Danielle Sharp was first in line!

Don opened the service door next to Tio's Tacos and started down the stairs, still thinking about Danielle. Of course, he knew her new ardor had a lot to do with his new status, but that was okay. Even if the glow wore off after a while, Don figured he'd never be a nobody again. People would always remember him as a lifesaver, a do-gooder—a hero. And Danielle would never have to be ashamed about hanging out with him anymore.

Walking along the loading dock platform, Don heard voices, which surprised him that late at night. He looked up and saw someone coming toward him. *Probably one of Tripp's new security gorillas*, he thought. Yeah, it is. He checked out the security uniform.

"All right, kid, what are you doing here, huh?" A guy as big as King Kong had his hand on Don's shoulder and was squeezing hard as he asked. Behind him, two others were loading something in front of the loading dock.

"Um, I'm just going for my bike," Don replied, trying his best to sound cool. "Would you mind letting go of me?" he asked. "My shoulder's a little sore."

But the man didn't let go. "Do we take him in?" he asked one of the other men at the truck.

"Let him go," the man replied.

The guy holding Don considered for a moment, and then turned him loose. "Okay, go get your bike," he growled finally. "But get out of here, kid—now."

"Okay," Don agreed. "Thanks." Turning around, he ran for his Harley as fast as he could. In no time, he was zipping away on his Harley, his heart racing a mile a minute, his mind churning.

He was thinking about that award he was going to collect the next day and, of course, Danielle. Seeing her, meeting her family, holding her in his arms—it had been his deepest dream come to life. And the dream wasn't over yet either. Danielle Sharp and Don James had a future—a long one, Don hoped. A very long one.

"Did you hear? There was another robbery last night! It was all stuff from Nick's dad's store too!" Patsy Donovan raced up to Lori, who was coming out of Tio's on her way to Don's award ceremony in the central plaza.

"I know! Nick came over and told me before," said Lori, a worried look on her face. "These thefts are really getting out of hand. Nick's father's going to lose a pile of money even with his insurance."

Just as the two friends were rounding the corner by Aunti Pasta's, Ann Larson popped up behind them. "Wait, you guys! I'm coming too!"

"Hi, Ann!" said Lori. "We were just talking about the robberies—"

"Isn't it awful!" said Ann as she fell in step with her friends. "Everyone's saying they need a new chief of security. The two guards they had watching last night were found tied up in a corner—some guards."

"Oh, look!" Lori cried happily when they came to the spot where the ceremony was being held. "Wow! The whole town turned out to see Don James get his award!" There was a small bandstand set up and the entire area was festooned with ribbons and flowers.

"Isn't it great!" exclaimed Patsy, taking the whole scene in.

"Look—there's Danielle!" said Ann, pointing to Lori's cousin, who was just walking by, wearing a bright red dress with a black patent belt. Danielle took a place in the first row right in front of the platform. She was followed by

Teresa and Heather. "I love that dress!" Ann added, a trace of envy in her voice.

"She does look fantastic! And she sure looks proud too," Lori observed. Lori turned and waved, but Danielle didn't notice her in the crowd.

"I wonder why she's so proud. She didn't save anybody's life!" Patsy said.

"Give her a break," chided Lori lightly. Lori knew that Danielle wasn't Patsy and Ann's favorite person in the world. She had pulled one or two stunts on them in the past that weren't exactly friendly. But they didn't know Danielle the way Lori did. They didn't know how vulnerable she was, and how hard she worked to maintain her image. Being Danielle Sharp required a lot of nerve and energy, thought Lori sympathetically.

The president of the Merivale Mall Merchants Association was on the dais tapping the microphone and droning, "Testing—one, two, three . . ." Then Lori saw Don with Danielle on his arm, chatting with little Eddie's radiantly happy mother and father. Little Eddie was too busy drinking a bottle of juice to care much about what was going on around him.

Don left Danielle and took his seat on the dais next to the mayor. Lori noticed how nervous he looked. He kept glancing at his feet whenever anyone came up to shake his hand. He seemed a little stiff and awkward in a suit, even though he looked wonderful in it.

Finally, the mall president cleared his throat and spoke into the microphone. "Ladies and gentlemen," he began. "Today we've gathered here to reward an act of heroism. It isn't often that we see one human being put his own life at risk so that another may live, but that is exactly what happened right here at our mall just a few days ago."

Everyone was staring at Don, who had his head bowed modestly now.

"Mayor, would you care to come up and give the award to this fine young man?" The audience applauded the mayor as he made his way to the microphone.

"Delighted!" the mayor began dramatically. "There's a lot of bad press about teenagers these days. It seems they can do nothing right. They're impolite, they have problems learning, they don't care. Yes, I've heard it all—but now there's Don James, a young man who has proven, by his heroism, just exactly what our young people are made of. Don, would you step forward please?"

Don made his way up to the podium, and the crowd went wild cheering.

"Well, son," the mayor said, "it gives me great pleasure to present you with his award. In this envelope you will find two checks. One is from the mall association, and the other is from the mayor's office. Together they total five hundred and fifty dollars."

The crowd broke into applause and Don's face turned bright red. "And now, Don," said the mayor, "would you care to say something?"

This seemed to throw Don. "Me?" he asked quietly as the mayor pushed him in front of the mike.

"Um—" began Don. "Well, I don't know what to say exactly—I guess—well, I'm just glad I could help. That's all."

Little Eddie's mother started the applause this time. Tears streaming down her face, she stood up and clapped enthusiastically. The others joined in, and Don, the reluctant hero, just stood waiting for it to be over.

Suddenly from the back of the crowd there was a commotion. Everyone turned and watched a red-faced Archie Tripp make his way through the crowd with four security guards. On the dais, Don looked worried.

Tripp stepped up to the podium. As the curious crowd watched, he walked over to the mayor and the mall association president.

"Sorry to break up the proceedings," he said loudly enough to be heard through the microphone. "But we have evidence that Don James is involved in the recent robberies here at the mall! It's our job to place him under arrest!"

CHAPTER NINE

Don! Under arrest? Danielle could hardly believe her eyes and ears. But unbelievable as it was, Archie Tripp was there, leading Don away.

"Wait a minute!" cried the mayor excitedly. "Are you sure you have the right person? This boy is a hero!"

Some people in the crowd started cheering for Don, but when Tripp faced them and waved his hands, they stopped. "I have proof—positive evidence!" Tripp declared.

"Baloney!" cried Don. His eyes were wild. Danielle could see the fear in them, and the hurt too. "You can't have proof, because I wasn't involved in those robberies! I'm not a thief—and I never have been!"

Danielle's blood began to boil at the way Tripp ignored Don's protest. The security chief turned to the mayor with a snide smile. "He was with them last night. We got it all on video tape."

"Why didn't you stop the robbery then?" someone in the crowd shouted to Tripp.

"Yeah!" another heckled. "Tell us who the others were."

"Well, we couldn't see their faces because they kept them down all the time," Archie answered.

Thank goodness some people were sticking up for Don, Danielle thought. If it weren't so awkward, she would too. But as Don's girlfriend, she thought it would be best to appear cool and collected. The last thing she wanted was her picture in the paper or anything like that.

"The reason we didn't nab him last night," Tripp explained to the man on the dais and to anyone else who was listening, "is that we looked at the tape only this morning."

"You guys are really swift," the first heckler shouted again. A giggle rippled through the crowd.

"Why weren't you and your men there?" someone logically asked.

Everyone laughed because they all knew Archie's guards had been conked out and trussed up like turkeys.

"Mr. Mayor, he's our boy," said Tripp matter-of-factly.

Horrified, Danielle watched as the mayor slowly shook his head. "This is a shock—" he murmured. "A shock." He stared at Don and shook his head one last time.

"Okay, let's go." Archie signaled his son Vince to take Don's arm. With a nasty smile the younger Tripp complied.

"Hold on a minute!" Don yelled, desperate. "You don't believe this bozo, do you? I didn't do anything wrong! I swear!"

But Don's protest didn't mean a thing to anyone on the dais. The mall association president looked embarrassed, and the mayor had resumed shaking his head.

"Calm down. Calm down. You can tell it to the judge," Archie Tripp muttered to Don. "Sorry, Mr. Mayor. Sorry, folks."

A buzz of excitement moved through the crowd, and the press lost no time getting a round of pictures.

Pop! Pop! Flash! The cameras were everywhere now. Poor Don could hardly make his way off the platform. But then it was over. As the crowd watched, Don was led to the back of the atrium, where two uniformed police were waiting for him.

After that the crowd broke up. The only thing anyone was talking about was what they'd just seen and Don James. Not many of them were convinced Don was innocent either. Tripp had been mighty convincing when he talked about his "positive evidence" against Don!

From her place in the front row, Danielle

turned around and frantically searched the crowd for a friendly face. Just moments earlier, she had been so proud, so happy. Now she was totally devastated.

"Danielle!" Lori's voice cut through the murmur of the scattering crowd. Sure enough. There was her cousin cutting through the crowd, trying to get close to Danielle.

"Oh, Lori," cried Danielle when her cousin finally reached her and threw her arms around her in a compassionate hug. "This is a total nightmare! I've got to get out of here right now! I can't stand this!"

Danielle grabbed Lori by the arm and started pushing through the crowd, her head down to avoid being recognized. Why, oh, why, had she worn a red dress? Now people were pointing to her and muttering that she was Don's girlfriend. Danielle thought she would die.

"But, Dani—we've got to help Don! We've got to go to the police and tell them what we know! Don is innocent and we can help prove it!"

Danielle and Lori had reached the back wall.

"Poor Don! *Nobody* believes him!" Danielle moaned, shaking her head in frustration and grief.

"But you were with him last night, Danielle," Lori cried. "You can help him!"

"How? I can give him an alibi only until the time they got his picture on that tape."

"But the tapes have the time printed on them and you can help him for part of the time," Lori insisted.

Fear shot straight up Danielle's spine. She *was* with Don the night before. She'd even dropped him off at the mall. Her car was probably on the outside security tape.

What if the police thought she was involved or something? She might even be sent to jail!

Just then Heather and Teresa came flying around the corner and smacked right into Danielle and Lori.

"Danielle!" Teresa shrieked. "Are you all right? After they took Don away, we couldn't find you!"

Teresa nodded briefly at Lori, who nodded back. Heather didn't even bother to nod. Her ice-blue eyes were riveted on Danielle, and there was a look of exaggerated pity on her face.

"Poor Danielle, you must be *so* embarrassed!" cried Heather.

"Embarrassed? Why should I be embarrassed?" Even as the words were coming out of her mouth, Danielle could feel the panic move up her. If everybody thought Don was guilty, that would make *her* the object of ridicule at Atwood!

"People are going to think you're a total lowlife!" Heather declared forcefully.

"Don't worry, Danielle," Teresa purred. "You can tell people you didn't really know him that well."

"What are you talking about? Danielle Sharp and Don James have been *the* item lately! Nobody'll believe her if she says that," Heather protested. "You'll have to make up some other kind of story, Danielle. You can say you never really liked him, but that he kept bugging you to go out with him, or something. Or that he held you hostage until you said yes."

Danielle looked over at Lori and took courage from her presence. "Cool out, you two!" Danielle chided. "Don is *not* going to get in trouble because he really didn't have anything to do with those robberies. I know, because it just so happens I was with him last night." Don just had to have his name cleared. He had to. Anybody who really knew him knew he was totally honest. That was another "best thing" about him!

"You were with him last night? Really? Where?" asked Teresa, her eyes widening.

"Oh, just riding around," Danielle lied. No way was she going to admit that she had been up at the Overlook with Don.

But still Teresa was looking at her as if she were from another planet. "Danielle," she said, "you're not defending him, are you? If you are, you're out of your mind!"

"Don't you realize what people will think if you stay involved with him?" Heather agreed.

"Really! Everybody thinks he's a criminal," Teresa insisted.

"He always was bad news," echoed Heather.

"You'll be a complete outcast! *Nobody* will associate with you anymore. I mean, *we* will"—Teresa looked unsure of what she was saying—"but, you know, *other* people—"

"Really, Danielle. Why don't you just forget him and get another boyfriend," said Heather. "Somebody normal."

Blinking back angry tears, Danielle threw a hard look at her so-called two best friends. Don James was such a better person than they were. And what kind of friend would she be to walk away from him now, when he needed her support! There was no way she could just drop Don now, not after what he'd come to be to her. So why did everything they were saying cut her like a knife?

"Don James is perfectly normal! In fact, he's wonderful!" She hadn't meant to sound so defensive—it had just come out that way.

"Well, whatever—" murmured Heather, arching an eyebrow. Heather seemed to be getting bored with the whole subject of Danielle and Don. "Listen, you guys, Facades got in a shipment of sequined sweat shirts that you'll die for. I want to get one before they disappear."

"Danielle—I'm going," said Lori. "Are you coming with me?"

Her heart pounding, Danielle looked from Lori to her friends. If she went off with Lori now, it would look as if she were choosing her cousin over Teresa and Heather. She couldn't do that, even if she wanted to. Atwood could be a very cold place without friends. She'd learned that her freshman year, before she'd gotten in with Teresa and Heather.

"Well—" Danielle drawled, looking from Lori to Teresa. She could always stop by the police station later. That way, she could help Don without turning Teresa and Heather against her. "I think I have to check out those sweat shirts too," she finally announced. "You take care, Lori, okay?"

Turning away from Lori so she wouldn't have to face her, Danielle breezed off with Teresa and Heather as if Don James and the trouble he was in didn't mean a thing to her. It was strictly a performance, but she had to make it believable.

"Dad—I *know* he's innocent. Danielle knows it too!" Lori looked over at her father, her eyes pleading to be understood.

"I believe you, Lori." George Randall shook his head regretfully and turned to the pantry to put away the small bag of groceries he had just brought in. "I saw him a few days ago at the garage with Mike. I overpaid him by mistake, and he came running after me with the extra money. A kid like that isn't a thief."

"See! Don's really a good kid, but people

always think the worst of him," Lori insisted, folding a brown paper bag and putting it under the sink. "He always is ready to help out, and he never puts other people down either. Don's a really good *person*."

"Weren't you his principal, George?" Lori's mother asked, walking to the refrigerator to take out salad makings.

"Yes," her dad answered. "And Lori's right. He always looked out for the little kids. He'd talk to them if they were shy, and he'd make sure they didn't run into the street. But even then, Don had a 'tough' act, as if he didn't care what people thought of him. I agree he's not a thief."

"He may not be a thief, but he's definitely in jail!" Lori exclaimed heatedly. "He has to post bail, and he doesn't have that kind of money." Lori threw herself against the utility closet door and let out a sigh.

"Hmmm—" said her father, sliding the pantry door shut. "I just got an idea. You know, your uncle Mike and I were talking about Don this morning. Apparently he's dating Danielle?" Her father shot a questioning look over at Lori.

"Well, sort of—" Lori said grudgingly. She was still steaming at Danielle's lack of loyalty to Don now that he was in trouble.

"Mike likes him," her father went on. "He said he was surprised Danielle was going out with someone as down to earth as Don, but he was delighted. Maybe if I give Mike a call—"

"Oh, would you, Dad?" Lori piped up. "One word from Uncle Mike and the police would let Don go in a minute!" Everyone in Merivale knew Mike Sharp. If he wanted to, Danielle's father could have run for mayor and won.

Lori's father wasted no time pushing the Sharps' number on the beige wall phone. "Mike? Hi, George here. Listen, have you heard about the trouble Don James has run into? Oh, you have. And? You are? Great. I'll meet you down at the station house. Fine."

Hanging up with a grin, Lori's father announced, "Mike's going down to pay Don's bail!"

"Hooray!" Lori couldn't help jumping up and down and applauding. Now that good old Uncle Mike was on the case, help was on the way!

CHAPTER TEN

Pulling the hood of her teal blue woolen jacket up over her hair, Danielle looked both ways as she walked up the steps to the police station on Monday morning. The early sunlight glinted off the marble banisters, and an icy breeze cut through the air.

She'd parked six blocks away in order to avoid being seen. The last thing she needed was for any of her Atwood friends to see her white BMW parked in front of the police station before school. As far as anybody at Atwood was going to know, she and Don James were a thing of the past.

"Hello," Danielle mumbled to the friendly-looking police officer behind the main desk. "Um, I—well, I might as well just tell you. I was with Don James the night he was supposed to be robbing the mall, um—"

"Excuse me, miss? Could you speak up?"

the officer said in what sounded like a loud voice.

Danielle looked around. Nobody was listening, thank goodness.

"I said I was with Don James the night he was supposed to be robbing the mall," she repeated, leaning in closer and saying every word distinctly. If the police officer asked her *where* she was, she'd just have to die.

"Don James! Well, well. That's very interesting." The police officer opened her top drawer and pulled out some forms. "Would you like to have a seat and I'll take your statement?"

"I guess so," Danielle looked down at the old-fashioned wooden chair next to the desk.

"Your name?" she asked, her pen poised.

"Do I really have to give my name?" Danielle's green eyes looked absolutely pained.

"I'm afraid so—" the officer answered with a look of compassion.

Danielle glanced around the room helplessly. What she saw through the main double glass doors made her blood run cold. Jane Haggerty was about to step into the station house!

Jane had her Atwood *Tattler* notebook out, and she looked determined. Danielle quickly threw her hood up over her head again.

If Jane ever found out that Danielle was there defending Don James, that would be it for Danielle having any friends for the rest of her natural life!

"Excuse me, my contact lens is bothering me. Where's the ladies' room?" Danielle asked suddenly, one hand shielding her face.

"It's right over there. First door on the left," the officer answered.

"I'll, um—I'll be right back," Danielle stammered. But when she stood up, she let her shoulders hunch over as if she were an old woman. Then she ambled away from the desk, watching Jane from the corner of her eye. When she was sure the junior reporter was involved with the police officer, Danielle broke free and flew down the steps of the police station. So much for justice!

Don James looked in the mirror over his chipped painted bureau and grimaced. The house was quiet. Everyone must have left for work already.

The past night had *not* been fun. He'd lain awake on the narrow cot in the jail and stared at the ceiling. He wondered if spending the night there would go on his record or anything.

Just two days earlier he'd been on top of the world, and now this had happened. The funny thing was, it was just like one of his nasty teachers used to tell him: "You'll wind up in jail someday." The teacher said it because Don liked to play with cap guns, but now it looked as if she were right.

The whole situation sent a cold shiver up

Don's back. Don had to admit it—he was scared, really scared. Archie Tripp and his son, Vince, really had a grudge against him. That was the worst part. If the chief of security wanted him behind bars—and if the real robbers weren't caught—well, *somebody* was going to be charged with those thefts. So why not Don James?

Don shut his eyes momentarily and winced. The worst part was that video tape. He hadn't seen it himself, but he knew enough to know that it was accurate. After all, he had been there the night of the robbery. And he knew now that the guys he thought were security officers were the robbers. And he had talked to them! Of course, when he tried to tell Tripp what that conversation was really like, the security chief had just laughed in his face. But couldn't they have seen that the one guy was holding him? Maybe the tape only panned and missed that section. *That must be it*, he decided.

Whew. Don blew out his cheeks and shook his head to try to clear his mind. Drawing a comb through his hair, he thought of the one bright spot in this whole mess—Danielle, and her family.

Don just assumed that Danielle had sent her father down to help him. And because she'd done that, he had a lawyer and a chance to beat the charges. *Thank goodness for Red*, he thought, a smile creeping into his lips in spite of everything. Danielle was so beautiful, so sweet, and now he was finding out just how loyal she was too.

Don looked over at the old electric alarm clock on the floor next to his mattress. Time to head out to school.

Jerry Friedman, the lawyer Mike Sharp introduced him to, had told him to go about his life as if this mess weren't happening, and that was exactly what he planned on doing.

Except for one thing—he had to see Danielle, to thank her for everything she had done. He'd drive over to Atwood Academy at lunchtime. And when he did, he was going to take her in his arms and give her a kiss that would tell her how much she meant to him—so she would never forget.

"Can you imagine?" Wendy Carter tittered. "There she was right in the front row, looking up at him with these adoring eyes, for heaven's sake! I was surprised she didn't offer to go to jail with him!"

Hiding in one of the stalls in an Atwood girls' room, Danielle didn't have to wonder who Wendy and her friends were talking about.

"All I can say is, she *never* had great taste in boys," Ashley Shepard was saying. Danielle could just picture Ashley standing in front of the mirror, pulling a brush through her silky blond hair with a look of total self-adoration.

"Oh! And did you see her run off with her cousin? The way she had her head down?" Danielle couldn't see Jane Haggerty's imitation, but it must have been hysterically funny—Wendy and Ashley were completely cracked up.

Danielle heard the outer door swing open again. When were they going to leave so she could get out of there?

"Hi, everybody." Danielle recognized Georgia Ross's whine instantly. "Oh, I love your lipstick, Ashley— By the way, did you guys hear the latest? Danielle Sharp's getting two years off for good behavior."

Danielle turned red right down to her toes as Wendy, Ashley, and Jane convulsed in laughter. *Ha, ha, Georgia,* thought Danielle—*very funny!*

After they'd all spent themselves in laughter, Wendy said, "Come on. I'm *starved,*" and in a minute the four were out the door. "Want to bet they still show up together at the Sadie Hawkins dance?" roared Ashley as they went. "Danielle was never short on nerve!"

The Sadie Hawkins dance! Danielle had almost forgotten it. Of course there was no way she could show up with Don now. She'd have to tell him as soon as she saw him again.

When the door fell shut, Danielle peeked out of the stall. She was alone. Walking to the mirror, she took out a lipstick and put a fresh coat of coral over her lips. *If* she ever got out of this mess, those girls would pay, Danielle vowed. Just the day before they had all been wishing they were her— And it could be that way again tomorrow.

But in the meantime, the only thing to do was starve the gossip monster. The truth was, no matter how much she cared about Don, she hadn't been out with him often. It wasn't as if Don were her *boyfriend* or anything. He was just somebody she knew. That was one way of looking at it, anyway, and that was how she was going to play it.

Walking along the hall to the cafeteria, Danielle held her head high and practiced her new attitude. But when she got to the entrance of the cafeteria, she could feel everyone looking at her. Well, all the more reason to look good. Danielle pulled her lips back in an enormous smile.

"Hi, Teresa! Hi, Heather!" she called to her friends, who were already at their usual table in the back of Atwood's lunch room. "So, what's happening around the big A? We're going to be dramatizing *The Canterbury Tales* in English. Isn't that a hoot!" she said when she got to the table.

No wonder Teresa and Heather looked confused. Danielle wasn't exactly famous for her enthusiasm about class projects.

"Danielle, do you realize the whole school has been talking about you all morning—" Heather informed her as Danielle slid into the seat.

"So?" asked Danielle, pretending not to care.

"I don't know what to say to anybody," said Teresa. "I mean, what a humiliation!"

"I don't know what the big deal is, Teresa. I hardly even know Don James," Danielle lied.

Heather and Teresa exchanged puzzled looks. With a laugh, Danielle leaned across the table. "Let them talk. It'll all die down soon enough," she said. Then she flashed them one of her thousand-watt smiles.

Ordinarily Teresa and Heather would have smiled back. But this time they just sat there with awful blank expressions on their faces. Were they going to turn on her too?

"I mean, it wasn't like he was my *boyfriend* or anything," Danielle insisted, reaching for a carton of pineapple juice.

Heather and Teresa still wore the same identical blank stares. Then suddenly the room became dead quiet—every voice in the cafeteria had been hushed. Only a single metallic bang from the kitchen punctured the silence.

As everyone turned as one to stare at the entrance, Teresa stammered, "Um, Danielle, I hate to tell you this. He's here!"

"What?" gasped Danielle. "Who?" It couldn't be the police, could it? Maybe they were coming for *her*? No, she hadn't done anything wrong—

"It's Don James!" whispered Heather frantically. "He's looking for someone! And my guess is—it's you."

Slowly turning her neck toward the entrance, Danielle saw him too. He was standing alone, scanning the room, untouched by all the eyes on him.

"I'm gone. If he asks, tell him I was out sick or something." With as much grace as possible, Danielle slid out from the table. Fortunately, the rear exit was right behind her. So much for lunch.

Danielle pulled into her driveway after school with a sigh of relief. The afternoon had been excruciating. Part of her felt like a dog for pretending that her relationship with Don meant nothing to her.

Of course, another part of her was perfectly comfortable with it. After all, she really didn't know Don *that* well. . . .

But her feelings did another flip-flop when she saw a Harley in her driveway.

It couldn't be—but it was. Danielle recognized the bike immediately. Trotting up to the house, she threw open the door and ran into the living room.

"Hi, darling." Her mother sounded so cheerful. There she was, totally relaxed, her legs tucked up under her and a cup of coffee in her hands.

"Don, this is just the kind of injustice that irks me," she was saying. "I promise, my husband and I will do everything we can to help."

"Thanks, Mrs. Sharp. I really appreciate it. I don't know what I'd do without you people."

His voice was so sincere, genuine, and so grateful. And when he turned to Danielle, she could feel her heart practically jump.

"Hi, Danielle. Well, I'd better go call Premier. Don, are you staying for dinner?" Mrs. Sharp asked.

"Well, thanks, Mrs. Sharp, if it's really no trouble—"

"No trouble at all. Danielle can keep you company while I call," answered her mother with a smile as she moved toward the kitchen. It was amazing how Don had brought out a whole new side to her mother, thought Danielle.

"Hi, beautiful," Don said with an appreciative smile the second they were alone.

"Hi, Don." Thank goodness she didn't have to hide her relationship with Don at home anymore.

"How's it going for you, Red? Those snobs giving you a hard time at Atwood?" he asked, his eyes full of concern.

Isn't that just like Don, thought Danielle, her heart melting. *He* was the one who'd been arrested, and here he was showing an interest in her!

"How's it going with *you* is the question," said Danielle.

"Thanks to your family, I'm doing okay. I sure am glad I took you up on that dinner," he said. "And I'm awfully sorry for the trouble I've caused."

"Oh, Don, don't be silly," Danielle said, choking on a tear. Oh, why did Don James have to be such a terrific person? If he wasn't, she could have just walked away from him. But there he was—so sweet and so gorgeous.

"Oh, Danielle, I don't know what I'd do without you." Danielle's knees went limp as he reached out for her and pulled her toward him.

"Oh, Don," she murmured, unable to stop herself from hugging him back.

And then, right there in her living room, he pulled her closer and pressed his soft lips against hers. He kissed her, and he kissed her, and he kissed her again. . . .

CHAPTER ELEVEN

"Lori, there's no sense in my trying to fool myself anymore. Even up at the Overlook, when I kissed him, his face was all tense. The best kiss of the night was a peck. I mean, it just goes to prove that Irving Zalaznick hates my guts. That's the beginning, the middle, and the end of it."

Patsy looked more forlorn than she had since she'd been pounds heavier and hadn't been able to get a date. She sat on the edge of her bed, staring blankly at the mirror over her vanity. "Why does he hate me, Lori?"

Just looking at her was breaking Lori's heart. "Patsy," said Lori. "You're being ridiculous, you know that, right? Irv Zalaznick doesn't hate you!"

"Okay, okay, he doesn't hate me. He just thinks I'm a horrible person, and doesn't want to go out with me!" Patsy agreed too quickly.

If she weren't acting so pathetic, Lori would

have laughed at her friend. "Patsy, you *know* Irv is crazy about you! He has been all year."

"Then what's going on?" Patsy moaned. "I practically had to drag him up to Overlook, and then it was all me, no him. I mean, *I* kissed him—"

"Yes?" encouraged Lori.

"But he didn't kiss me back! It was so humiliating, I could have died. Today I had lab with him and I couldn't even look at him. He probably thinks I go around kissing people all the time!" Now Patsy was lying on her bed facedown. "I want to run away—"

"Maybe he's scared that he's not a good kisser or something." So saying, Lori leaned an elbow on the vanity Patsy used for a desk.

For a second Patsy's eyes flickered with hope, then she plopped back down on the bed. "That's not it," she murmured. "He used to kiss me all the time. He knows he's a good kisser. Of course, that was when he *liked* me."

Lori shook her silky blond hair and shut her eyes in frustration. This silly conversation had been going around in the same circle for an hour, and Patsy was still caught up in it.

Of course Lori knew that it wasn't silly to Patsy—not at all. And she was trying her best to help her friend.

Why *had* Irv Zalaznick suddenly stopped all activity in the romance department? Lori had been racking her brains about it all night, and the only thing she could come up with was fear. Yet, whenever she told Patsy what she thought, Patsy waved the idea away.

"He knows I like him. He knows I want him to kiss me. He isn't afraid, I can tell—oh, no! I just thought of something horrible!" Patsy had covered her face with her hands and let out a stifled scream.

"What? What?" asked Lori, full of concern.

"Maybe he likes another girl? Diane Elliot or Sue Walters? Oh, no! I bet that's it! I bet he likes someone else!"

"Patsy, control yourself!" The idea of Irv Zalaznick and anyone but Patsy Donovan was too funny for words. "I can't believe you!" Lori took in her friend with a tiny shake of her head and a wry grin. "You're really off the deep end with that one, Pats—sorry."

Patsy's lip was trembling and her reddish-brown curls were beginning to shake and tumble like autumn leaves. "Well, then, Lori, answer me this, why doesn't he like to kiss me anymore?"

"Oh, Patsy—" Lori sighed. "I wish I could tell you. I mean, I know he likes you. There must be something else going on in his life. Maybe he's upset about something."

Everything Lori was saying felt so inadequate. Patsy was still there, her chin trembling, her eyes filling with tears. Lori felt totally helpless.

And when her eyes glanced at the pink

clock behind Patsy's bed, a pang of fear shot through her. It was already ten of ten!

"Oh, no! I have to go home right away," Lori sputtered, reaching for her coat. "If I don't leave right now, I'll be late!"

"Oh, Lo-ori—" Patsy's sobs were coming now, great gulping sobs. There was no way Lori could walk out then. Some things were more important than others. And friendship was way up there on Lori's list.

"Patsy, don't cry. It'll work out. You'll see—" Standing up and reaching over to give her friend a hug, Lori tried not to think about her curfew.

"Please don't go, Lor—" Patsy begged.

"Well, let me call my folks, okay?" Lori reached for the old-fashioned black phone hidden under Patsy's bed. The line was busy.

"Lori—do you think it's my hair? Maybe I should get it straightened? Or maybe I should cut it all off? Maybe a radical move would get his attention."

Getting Patsy in a better frame of mind took some doing. By the time Lori actually left the Donovan home, it was a quarter *after* ten. She knew she had blown it—royally.

Her feelings sinking, Lori drove home. No way was she going to make it to Rob Matthews's party with Nick.

Her mother didn't say a word when Lori walked in at ten-thirty. She just gave Lori a look.

"Wait, Mom," said Lori, taking her coat off and hanging it in the hall closet. "I had to stay! Patsy was really upset and I couldn't just walk out on her!"

"It's always something, isn't it, Lori? But a deal is a deal—and you have just broken your end of the bargain."

"I agree," said her dad, who'd been listening quietly from his chair in the living room.

Oh, why were they being like this? The whole curfew thing had come between them in the most awful way!

"I tried to call!" Lori protested.

"Well, I was talking on the phone for quite a while," her mother confessed.

"I was going to tell you what was going on. I mean, I know you guys want me to be a good friend to Patsy, don't you?"

How could they say no? Everyone in the Randall household liked Patsy. They'd all spent a lot of time together.

"Well, we'll let it go this time, Lori, but one more time and you're out." There wasn't much give in her mother's position, and one look at her dad convinced Lori he was in complete agreement.

"There won't be another time. You'll see." Lori was positive. She would show them. If she was going to get to stay out a half-hour later the night of Sadie Hawkins, she *had* to show them!

CHAPTER TWELVE

Ugh. Collapsed on her bed, Danielle didn't even notice the silky feel of the satin comforter that she had crumpled in her hand. She stared past the white wall and heaved an enormous sigh.

Oh, why was her life so awful? For four agonizing days at Atwood, she had been pretending that Don James didn't mean a thing to her. Then, after school, she'd come home and pretend that her social status at Atwood didn't mean a thing to her.

Much more of it and she'd go bananas—definitely! The situation was out of hand, and Danielle was fast coming to the conclusion that leading two lives was impossible.

The worst part was that she felt like such a rat too. Her acting ability at school was just fantastic. Nobody at Atwood—not even Teresa or Heather—even remotely suspected that she still cared about Don, let alone that she was still seeing him! If they ever found out, they'd be mortified. That's why Danielle had been dedicating her life to making sure they *never* found out.

Ever since the award ceremony, Danielle had not been seen with Don outside of her house. In fact, making excuses to him about why she couldn't go out had become draining. If she had to invent one more imaginary homework project, she'd throw up.

She had avoided going anywhere alone too. The less she was around, the less people could speculate about her life. But she was finding out that staying home could be incredibly boring— especially that afternoon. Don couldn't come over.

Don . . . Flipping over on her side, Danielle let out another giant sigh. As much as she hated to think of it, things had changed between them over the past couple of days.

Don was so bummed out. All he wanted to do was talk about *the case*. He was constantly powwowing with her father and his lawyer. Then he'd tell her all the little details about it, what the law said, and what his defense was going to be. And on and on. It was all so boring—especially since Danielle had come to the sad conclusion that it really didn't matter whether he won or lost.

True, if he won, Don wouldn't have to go to

jail. But he'd still be finished, socially speaking—as far as she was concerned anyway. Kids at Atwood had long memories, and they weren't forgiving. Once something horrible happened to a person, it wasn't forgotten.

Then there was the Sadie Hawkins dance. She still hadn't told Don she didn't want him to go with her. As far as he knew, she didn't care what the people at Atwood thought of him. He was still under the impression that they were going to meet at the academy on Saturday night!

Every time she tried to break it to him, she just looked into those gorgeous eyes of his and all her courage and resolve melted. How was she ever going to get the nerve to tell him she didn't want to go with him? Just thinking of it now gave her a hollow feeling in the pit of her stomach.

It was all so unfair too! Don was a better person than almost anybody at Atwood! If he were rich, they'd all be after him.

Danielle leaned back on the pillows and reminded herself of the facts. Don James wasn't rich. He was a nobody who lived outside of town, went to public school, worked in a gas station, and was accused of being one of the robbers at the mall. If she were really smart, she'd just forget him.

Sitting up, Danielle reached over for the new issue of *Glitz* that had just come in the mail. Flipping listlessly through the pages, she shook her head sadly. If only life were like a fashion magazine . . .

A spread on spring sweaters in soft pastel shades caught her eye. The sweaters in the magazine were probably just like the ones Teresa had been talking about at lunch. At Facades the whole spring line had come in. And the clothes they were showing were the most interesting to hit the shops since she was a freshman.

The mall. That's where she wanted to be! And she knew exactly what she wanted to be doing right now. Shopping. Hanging out. Being seen.

Just the thought of Facades or To the Manor Born was enough to make her crave the familiar. She could be with Heather and Teresa at O'Burgers, or taking an aerobics class at the Body Shoppe. Better, she could indulge in something chocolate and gooey at Cookie Connection.

The mall. She'd been avoiding it for four whole days, but enough was enough. After all, she'd done a spectacular job of convincing her friends she didn't care a bit about Don James. She'd done so well that people had already started gossiping about Georgia Ross and some boy from Merivale High. . . .

The mall. If she went there, she could get her mind off everything.

Half an hour later Danielle smiled at her reflection in the window of Hobart Electronics

on her way to the main atrium. Coming to
the mall had been the perfect thing to do.
The minute she'd started walking down the
corridor past the stone benches and graceful
potted trees, all thoughts of Don and the robberies, and Atwood Academy, had flown from
her head.

This was so much better than staying home
sulking. After all, what good was being gorgeous and classy and tremendously witty unless you got to flaunt it?

Now, to find Heather and Teresa, she thought,
stepping confidently onto the escalator for the
fourth floor.

They were probably in Facades. Danielle
stepped off on the fourth level and walked the
familiar route to Facades. Peeking through the
window, she broke into a grin. Yep, there they
were, holding up some cashmere sweaters that
were out of this world.

Danielle made straight for the door. But
before she got there she saw Don James coming
up on the escalator. What was *he* doing on the
top floor? A shudder went through her body.
He's looking for me, she realized. Glancing desperately inside Facades, Danielle saw Teresa and
Heather making their way to the entrance. Unless she did something, and fast, she and Heather
and Teresa and Don James would all collide
right there! Total disaster!

Thinking fast, Danielle pulled her coat collar up and backed quickly away and around a corner. Seeing that the door of the janitor's closet was open, she ducked inside and pulled the door closed behind her.

This is just great, she thought bitterly. *The cameras are probably recording me right this second.* She could just see Archie Tripp's face when he watched the security tape the next day. *Say, isn't that the girl Don James was hanging around with? What's she doing hiding in that closet?* Danielle had a clear vision of herself in a prison uniform.

A few minutes passed. Was it safe to come out? Danielle peeked out the door. There was no sign of Don, but Heather and Teresa were just coming around the corner, laden with packages. "Danielle!" shrieked Teresa. "What are you doing there?"

Danielle raised an eyebrow and tossed her friend a little smile. "Shopping. Is that so incredible?"

"Shopping inside a service closet?" asked an incredulous Teresa.

"I was just fixing my lipstick," Danielle answered saucily. She could tell Teresa didn't believe her.

"I thought you had that big French assignment," said Heather, shifting her packages for better distribution.

"Oh, I finished it," Danielle lied. "Are you going downstairs?" Teresa nodded and Danielle quickly fell in step with her friends.

"So? Who's it going to be, Danielle?" Teresa asked slyly as the three girls headed for the elevator. "I hear Keith Canfield doesn't have a date yet. Neither does Freddy Hamilton."

With that, Heather cracked up. Keith Canfield and Freddy Hamilton had to be Atwood's two biggest losers. "Oh, leave poor Danielle alone. She'll find someone to take to Sadie Hawkins. Won't you, Danielle?"

"All the good ones are already taken," Teresa sniffed. "Too bad you wasted all that time with that Don James."

"Oh, well," Danielle tossed off lightly. "I'm on the dance committee. I don't have to bring a date." Thank goodness she had worn enough blusher to cover any real blush. Her cheeks were burning.

"Rob Matthews is so sweet," Heather sighed, suddenly changing the subject. "His party is going to be so incredible. I'm helping him plan it."

"Are you two up for something to eat?" Danielle suggested. "I have a real craving for something gooey."

"Not me," said Teresa without hesitation. "I have to get home for a fitting of my gown. My mom's seamstress is coming over."

"I'm going to go over to Rob's," said Heather with a couple of hundred stars in her eyes. "We're meeting with his caterer. Sorry, Danielle."

"Oh, well, that's okay," murmured Danielle,

trying to hide her disappointment. "I think I'm going to do some shopping anyway."

"What are you wearing to the dance?" Heather asked innocently when they reached the first level.

"I'm not sure yet," Danielle answered her. Apparently the Sadie Hawkins dance was all anybody could think about.

"Well, bye, Dani—" said Heather. "Should I tell Rob you'll be coming to the party?"

"I'm not sure yet."

"Maybe you can invite Ryan Roper." Heather was trying to be helpful, but Danielle wrinkled her nose. Ryan Roper wasn't exactly her type. Nice as he was, Danielle didn't go for guys with skin problems.

"Don't worry. I'll figure it out," said Danielle, forcing a smile. "In fact, I have someone in mind," she lied. "But you two better get going. I'll see you tomorrow."

"Okay, Danielle," said Teresa. And with a wave, her two friends were gone.

This insanity had to stop. She *had* to find Don right now and tell him they weren't going to the dance! She'd just have to beg off—give him some reason—any reason—why she had to break the date.

Holding her head high, and with a look of determination, Danielle set off in the direction of Video Arcade.

She practiced her lie all the way. She'd tell

him that her sister Christine had invited her to Kensington College for the weekend and that it had been arranged for months and that she'd forgotten about it and that she had to go. Don didn't know anybody at Atwood well enough to find out the truth. But he did know her parents. *Oh, well,* if he thought she was gone, he wouldn't call.

With a gulp, she saw the blinking lights of the arcade. It was now or never. Sure enough, there he was, standing at the Star Command machine. He was staring into its screen, and it looked as if he were trying to concentrate, but he looked awfully worried and distracted.

"Hey, Red." He smiled when he saw her.

"Sorry to break up your game," Danielle apologized.

"Oh, that's okay, I wasn't doing so hot anyway. My concentration's shot," he replied. "I'm glad you came by to see me. I was up at Facades trying to find you before."

"Oh. Well, um. Here I am," Danielle said. "Actually, I need to talk to you about something—"

"Yeah?"

"Um, see, something came up, and um, I'm not going to be able to go to the dance after all. I hope you didn't already rent your tux and everything."

Don cast his eyes down at the floor and took a deep breath. "Gee," he said softly, looking into her eyes. "What happened?" There was hurt and anger in his eyes.

Danielle launched into the speech she had rehearsed all the way to the arcade. "Um, well. See, Christine invited me to Kensington College to spend the weekend with her, and I feel like such a jerk about it, but I said I'd go, and then it slipped my mind totally! I'm so sorry, but my father handed me the plane ticket this morning, and—"

"Wait a minute. Your mother told me that your sister is in London for two weeks," he said slowly and pointedly.

Oops! Danielle had totally forgotten! "Oh, well, she didn't go. Her trip was canceled at the last minute." Her face was burning from the lie, and she could tell Don saw right through her.

"It's okay, Red," he finally said. "I understand—you're afraid to be seen with me."

The truth sounded so awful, Danielle couldn't possibly admit it. "Oh, no, Don! It's not that—it's not that at all! It's just—"

"Same old story, huh, Red?"

Danielle stared at him. "What do you mean?" she asked.

"My fault, really. I just convinced myself that you'd changed. But you haven't. You're still the same snob you always were. I was good enough for you when I was a big hero, but now that I'm just me again, well . . ."

"Don James, how can you say such a thing?"

Her indignant attitude was one hundred percent manufactured, but Danielle was hoping it would put Don on the defensive. "Do you realize that I actually went down to the police station to try to help you out?"

Don shook his head and nodded. "It's okay, Red, I still like you. You don't have to prove anything to me. Everybody has faults. You can't help it if you're a snob."

Danielle was blushing from her forehead to her chin now. "D-Don," she sputtered, but she didn't know what else to say. For once, words failed her.

Don remained still, his eyes never straying from hers. Danielle felt about two inches high. "I'm not stupid, you know, in spite of what people might say about me," he went on, his jaw set. "Do you think I didn't notice when you started hanging out with me at your house and nowhere else? I wasn't born yesterday, Red. Not even the day before yesterday." As much as he tried, he couldn't hide the hurt in his eyes. "All right. I'll skip the dance. It's no big deal. I got more important things to worry about anyway. Excuse me."

And with that, he turned back to his game, shoved two quarters into the slot, and banged hard at the control buttons.

Danielle turned slowly and walked away, feeling as lousy as she'd ever felt in her life. Why, oh, why, did Don have to get arrested, just when things were going so great? And why couldn't the stupid Sadie Hawkins dance have been *last* Saturday instead of this Saturday?

Life is so cruel, thought Danielle as she passed through the door. If only Don would understand. She hadn't meant to hurt his feelings. In fact, she'd been trying to *spare* them! How come he couldn't see that?

CHAPTER THIRTEEN

Danielle sat alone at the corner table in the back of Cookie Connection, staring at her melting death-by-chocolate sundae. She hadn't even touched it.

I understand—you're afraid to be seen with me. The image of poor Don standing in Video Arcade telling her that just wouldn't go away. In all the time she had known him, Danielle could never remember Don appearing so doleful.

It's okay, Red, I still like you. Only Don. Only Don could be that sweet. He'd really tried to let her off the hook gracefully.

Danielle stirred the gooey mess with her spoon. Instead of being relieved about having gotten out of going to Sadie Hawkins, Danielle felt worse than ever. Was she really such a disloyal creep? She seemed like one to herself.

"Er, excuse me, miss. Are you done?" Joe Murphy was bending over her.

"What time is it?"

"We close in ten minutes, miss. It's nine-twenty. The whole mall will be packing it in for the night."

Danielle nearly fainted. She'd been sitting there for hours! Quickly she paid her check and left.

Shaken, Danielle began wandering aimlessly down the promenade. There had to be someone she could talk to. There just had to be. But who? Teresa and Heather didn't understand. Not really.

Tio's Tacos. The bright orange flashing neon sign on the ground level caught Danielle's eye as she was wandering out of the mall. Of course—*Lori.*

Stifling a sob, Danielle pushed the wide glass door open and scanned the room. When she saw Lori, she couldn't help breaking out in a small smile despite her tears. There was Lori, up to her elbows in taco sauce as usual. Well, not literally, but she was filling about fifty red plastic containers with the stuff.

"Danielle!" Lori's face brightened when she noticed her cousin.

"Hi, Lor," Danielle said as cheerfully as she could. "Got a minute?"

"I will if you can hold on a sec. We're starting to close up. Have a seat, I'll be right with you. Want a taco? There're still one or two on the grill—"

"Um, no thanks." Danielle was not the least bit hungry, and even if she had been, Tio's Tacos wouldn't have been her choice. She took a seat in the corner and waited patiently while Lori finished her task.

"Okay," said Lori about three minutes later, crossing over to Danielle and taking off her Day-Glo yellow Tio's Tacos apron. "What's the problem?"

"Oh, Lori." Danielle sighed, her head in her hands. "It's a long, long story—"

"Uh-oh," Lori said, biting her lip. "I've got only a couple of minutes, Dani. I've got a curfew, and I can't afford to blow it."

Was Lori *rejecting* her? It couldn't be! Lori had always had time for Danielle. That's the way it had always been, ever since they were little kids. "But, Lori," she said pointedly, "this is *important*."

"Gosh, Dani, so's my getting home on time. I've already blown it once. It'll mean real trouble for me if I'm late again."

Danielle didn't mean to sob then, the tears just poured out. But when she started, she could see the instant effect it had on her cousin.

"Wait," said Lori. "I have an idea. I've got to go downstairs to put back these supplies. How about walking with me?"

Danielle considered the offer for a moment. It was better than nothing, she decided, especially since she had no one else to turn to. "Oh, all right." She sighed and followed Lori out the back door of the restaurant and down the stairs to the basement level.

"Is it about Don?" Lori asked gingerly as they made their way down.

Danielle was surprised. "How did you know?" she asked. "Am I that obvious?"

Lori laughed. "No," she replied. "Just a lucky guess. What's the matter? He's out on bail, isn't he? And he's sure to get acquitted at the trial—if there even *is* a trial—"

"It's not that," Danielle said, correcting her. "I was just awful to him, Lori. I rejected him completely, and now I think he's really gone. He'll never even talk to me again. And I don't blame him!"

Lori stopped at the bottom of the steps and turned around. "What?" she asked. "I can't believe that. What happened? Don's crazy about you. He always has been."

"But I really blew it this time with Don. I backed out of taking him to the Sadie Hawkins dance because I was afraid of what my friends would think. I made up a big story and he saw through the whole thing. He called me a snob— and he's right!"

"No wonder you're upset," Lori said sympathetically as she reached the locker marked Tio's and opened it.

"But how could I have brought him to Atwood, Lori? I'd be laughed out of the place!"

Lori stuffed the supplies in the locker and headed for the stairs again. From the look on Lori's face, Danielle could tell her cousin didn't really understand.

"Lori, Atwood's a very competitive place. It's not like public school, you know. And now I don't even have a date for the Sadie Hawkins dance. I'm a complete failure, Lori."

Lori sighed and turned to her cousin. "Danielle Sharp, you are the foxiest girl at Atwood Academy. Are you telling me you can't find a guy to invite to the Sadie Hawkins dance?"

Danielle's jaw crumpled. "I don't *want* another guy," she sniffed. "I want Don!"

"Aw, Dani—" Lori gave her cousin a big hug. "Maybe you should just hang in there. You know, seek him out and be nice to him, but lay off anything heavy for a while. Let time heal things. If he really cares about you, and if you really care about him, you'll find each other again. I predict that if you're patient, Don'll come around."

Danielle couldn't help smiling. *Thank goodness for Lori—sweet, sensible Lori.*

Lori looked at her watch. "Oh, gosh!" she cried, a look of alarm spreading over her face. "My curfew! If I want to stay at the Sadie Hawkins dance, I've got to fly!" She took the stairs two at a time. Danielle had to huff to keep up with her.

Rushing back into the restaurant, Lori looked around, amazed. The place was empty! Everyone must have gone home for the night.

"Oh, no!" Confirming her worst suspicion, Lori ran to the entrance and pressed herself against the heavy glass. "We're locked in! Ernie must have thought I'd gone home!"

"What?" gasped Danielle. "You mean we're stuck here overnight?"

Lori thought for a second. "No," she realized. "We can go out through the loading area downstairs. Come on!"

And once again they flew downstairs to the service area, Lori leading the way. But when she threw open the door at the bottom of the steps, and stepped into the underground area, she froze.

"Lori?" said Danielle softly, stepping toward her cousin.

"Dani, the door! Hold it open," Lori whispered frantically. But it was too late. The stairway door up to the mall clicked shut.

Danielle reached for the knob and tugged. "It won't open!" she complained.

"I know, after closing it locks automatically," Lori moaned softly.

"What's wrong?" Danielle placed a hand on her cousin's slender shoulder and gulped with fear. Three burly men were loading cartons onto the back of a truck about fifty feet

away. Tied up at their feet were two men in
mall security uniforms. They looked as if they
were out cold.

She and Lori had just stumbled onto the
mall robbers, and now they were locked in with
them!

CHAPTER FOURTEEN

"Tell me this isn't happening. Tell me it's just a bad dream," Danielle whispered hoarsely into Lori's ear. The robbers might look up at any moment and see them, and then they'd be in big trouble.

Lori bit her lip nervously, her gaze darting around the dimly lit loading dock. If only there were some way out! She grabbed her petrified cousin by the arm and pulled her behind a bunch of big boxes. "They won't be able to see us here—"

Looking furtively at the robbers, Lori vowed to memorize their faces. The robbers couldn't keep them averted from her.

"Oh, Lori, I'm so scared." Danielle looked small next to the large corrugated box she was huddled behind. "I mean, my life is screwed up enough, without getting killed in my prime—"

"Don't think like that," Lori replied. But her heart was beating wildly too.

"But, Lor, how are we going to get out of here?"

Lori surveyed the area. The only exit was the one right past where the thieves were standing. There was no way they could use that one.

"Well," Lori said as calmly as she could. "We'll just have to think of something. Right now we might as well be patient, because we're not going anywhere."

"Help us out, Louie! This thing weighs a ton!" The shortest thief was struggling with his end of a huge crate that was stamped Furniture-to-Go.

"That must be a sofa or something," whispered Danielle.

"Well, they have plenty of room for other stuff too," said Lori. The thieves' truck was one of the largest she'd ever seen, an oversize red and white moving van.

"All this comes with us." Louie was pointing to the line of boxes in front of the loading bays. "Don't forget—we're cleaning out tonight."

"All right, Louie," the third man answered. "But that means we're going to be here awhile." He wore a knitted cap over his scraggly black hair.

"We got a lookout, man, so don't worry," Louie snarled back.

So much for her curfew, thought Lori. She

could just picture her parents at home, steaming. She'd probably have a nine-thirty weekend curfew until she moved out of her house to go to college. But even that didn't seem so bad anymore. She'd be happy just to get out of there alive!

"Here's our lookout now, in fact." Louie chuckled.

Lori craned her neck. Coming across the dock to meet the thieves, a broad smile on his face, was none other than Vince Tripp! He was wearing a gray security uniform too. So—it was Archie's own son who was in with the thieves, the very guy who had roughed up Don and accused *him* of being the lookout!

"How we doing, Vinnie?" Louie wanted to know. "Any action out there?"

"Nope," Vince answered. "Very quiet. You know, this is getting to be downright easy."

Louie was chuckling. "Yeah, not bad. Not bad at all."

"I heard Hobart's is getting another shipment in on Friday," Vince offered.

"Oh, yeah?" Louie's eyes widened.

"Forget it, Louie! This is my last trip, know what I mean?" the short man muttered. "We're pushing our luck as it is!"

"Shh!" Louie chided. "Be quiet, will you, turkey!"

"It's okay," said Vince. "I'm telling you, the place is dead. Everyone's gone and I shut off the whole system." He pointed up at the cameras. "I'm going to tell them there was a power outage."

"Oh, yeah, they'll really believe that," the little man muttered under his breath.

"Of course they will! It's only my dad I've got to convince, remember? You think he won't believe his own son?"

"Hey, you guys! Get over here!" The third man had wandered down to a far loading bay. "What are we doing with this stuff?"

"What is it?" Louie called.

"Bunch of stuff marked Facades," was the answer.

"Forget it. That's just clothes," said the man with the scraggly hair.

"Says here they're leather coats," the third man called back.

"Let's take a look," said Louie, ambling over with Vince and the short man.

Lori and Danielle couldn't see the men anymore, but they could hear them.

"Open them up. We got to save space. We got a lot of stuff to take and we don't want to get stuck with a bunch of junk," Louie was saying.

"That's going to take an hour!" the short man protested.

"So?" replied Louie. "You got other plans for tonight? Start packing!"

"Dani, here's our chance." Lori was peering over a big box toward the exit. "If we're quiet, we might be able to make it to the exit without them seeing us."

"You think so, Lori?"

"It's a shot. What do you say?" asked Lori.

Danielle's green eyes met Lori's blue ones with a look of pure fire. "I think we should get out of here," whispered Danielle. "And I also think these guys should get what they deserve! Let's go!"

"If this doesn't work out, tell Nick I said I love him, okay?" said Lori as the two cousins crept out of their hiding spot and ventured down the long row of loading bays.

Danielle grabbed Lori's hand and gave it a warm squeeze. "We better be really quiet now," she warned.

"Ah, who's going to buy coats that look like that? I say, let's forget it," the short man was insisting loudly.

"Vince, you go back and keep watch. As for you, Shorty, you're getting your cut on this caper, so just do what I say," the head man growled. "Empty out this whole load. Ralph, you help him. Just put it all on these hand trucks."

"Danielle!" Lori mouthed the words desperately, because Danielle had stopped beside the robbers' truck.

"I'm coming—but first," Danielle whispered back, "I have to do something." With a devious wink Danielle swung into the open cab of the moving van. There was a tiny *ping*, and the hood of the van opened slightly. In a flash Danielle was under the hood, sticking her perfectly manicured fingers into the engine.

"This hose was the one that was giving Nick all that trouble, wasn't it?" she said, a wicked gleam in her eye as she flipped a hose out of the engine. "Or was it this one? Or this one?" In short order, there were two more hoses in Danielle's hand.

"Hurry! Vince is coming this way!" Lori whispered hoarsely.

"Coming," said Danielle, pushing the hood down gently. But on the way down it squeaked— loudly. Fear shot through Lori.

"Hey? What was that?" Vince asked.

"Check the truck," Louie shouted nervously.

"Danielle!" cried Lori, trying to get her cousin to hurry. In her panic Danielle threw the hoses on the floor. They landed with a sickening thud.

"Hey!" yelled Vince. "Someone's here!"

"Two girls!" shouted the short robber.

"Get them, Vince!" Louie commanded.

"Oh, no," muttered Lori, breaking into a sprint. "Danielle, hurry!" The exit was near, but the closer they got, the farther away it seemed.

"I'm running as fast as I can," Danielle said breathlessly. "These stupid heels—"

Turning back, Lori saw Vince coming up on Danielle. Just a few more seconds and he would be close enough to grab her! But Danielle surprised her cousin. She looked back at Vince and shrieked. Then with a start she doubled her speed, running like lightning toward the exit.

"They must have seen us!" the scraggly-haired man shouted. "They can identify us."

"I'm getting out of here!" cried the short robber.

"Me too!" yelled Louie, running to the truck.

"Wait! What about *me*?" cried Vince pathetically.

"You handle those girls!" yelled Louie, climbing up into the van and turning the key. But the engine only made the same sick sound Nick's had made up at the Overlook.

Vince speeded up. He was closing in on Danielle. Lori heard Danielle growing breathless and started to slow down. They had to escape! From somewhere deep inside herself Lori conjured up one more tiny iota of strength. Desperately she grabbed hold of Danielle's arm and dragged her cousin up the exit ramp. They burst out of the open double doors only half a dozen steps ahead of Vince Tripp.

"The fire alarm!" cried Danielle, breathlessly. "Pull it!"

Lori grabbed the red lever and tugged as hard as she could. Immediately a piercing siren began echoing through the empty mall. Vince, who had just come through the open doors, turned back, making for the truck, a look of sheer panic in his eyes.

By the time Vince reached them, two of the robbers were out of the cab, one kicking the tires and cursing, the other frantically working under the hood.

But it was too late. The call was already out at the Merivale police and fire departments, and help was on the way. Thanks to Lori's fast-thinking cousin, those robbers weren't going anywhere—except to prison!

CHAPTER FIFTEEN

"The robbers!" Lori shouted to the police when they arrived two minutes later.

"They're in there by the moving van!" added Danielle, pointing to the loading docks.

"Thanks, ladies!" the officer shouted without stopping. "Over here! Come on!" he yelled to the dozen police who were heading for the docks.

"Wow," exclaimed an excited Danielle. "They aren't kidding around, are they?"

Lori and Danielle crept back in and watched as the first officer ran up to the robbers, his gun drawn. Immediately the thieves threw up their hands. "Don't shoot!" cried the terrified short man. Louie looked tired and resigned, and Lori could see that Vince Tripp was shaking all over.

"I caught them red-handed!" Vince lied.

"Who are you trying to kid?" the scraggly-haired man blurted out.

"He's the lookout!" shouted Danielle from the safety of the ramp, where she and Lori were standing.

"You're under arrest—all of you," the first officer announced loudly as they cuffed the four thieves.

"You have the right to remain silent, you have the right to—" As the first officer read the criminals their rights, Lori turned to Danielle, and the two cousins collapsed into each other's arms.

"Oh, Lori—" Danielle sighed, giving her cousin the biggest hug ever. "We're safe!"

"Dani, you were fantastic!" Now that their ordeal was over, tears of relief fell down their cheeks.

"Thanks to you. Without you I would have walked right into those guys," Danielle said, choking back more tears.

"Are you the ones who set off the alarm?" Police Chief Adams beamed from ear to ear as he walked up the ramp toward them.

Lori nodded, and Danielle brushed a tear off her face. Suddenly they found themselves laughing, all the tension and anxiety falling away in a fit of giggles.

"She pulled the alarm," Danielle managed to say. "I disabled their van."

Adams raised an eyebrow, obviously impressed. "Do you realize that you two accomplished tonight what our entire police force hasn't been able to do? This is rich. Two teenage girls come along and wrap up the whole case for us."

"Just glad we could help," Lori said modestly.

"I'm impressed, very impressed. Well, it's late, girls. We can take care of the paperwork tomorrow morning. Do either of you need a lift home?"

"No thanks, our cars are out in the lot," Danielle answered.

"My assistant will get your names and addresses and we'll be in touch tomorrow bright and early. But now, head home and get yourselves a good rest. After tonight, you deserve it. Pete?" Turning to his assistant, the chief of police tipped his hat in Lori and Danielle's direction and went down to join the others.

"Please give me your names and addresses," said the chief's assistant, his pen out.

After all the information was given, Lori and Danielle walked out into the cool night air.

"Well, Lor," said Danielle as they walked to their cars, "next time you want to catch some thieves, give me a call, okay?"

"Wait till my mom and dad hear about this. They're going to flip," said Lori with a giggle. "This is definitely the most unique reason I've ever had for being late!"

"It was exciting, but let's not ever do it again, okay?" said Danielle, who had spotted her white BMW on the other side of the deserted parking lot. "Get home safely, Lor."

"I will. Bye, Dani—" With a wave and an affectionate look Lori headed for her old Spitfire.

Everything seemed so calm and so ordinary as she unlocked the door and climbed in. Just a few minutes ago her very life had been in danger!

With a grin she started the engine and pulled out of the lot for home. Nick was going to be so impressed. Everyone would be! And best of all, now that the real robbers were caught, Don James could finally put this whole nasty episode behind him.

The first thing Lori noticed when she turned onto her block was that the lights in her house were burning brightly. Obviously, her parents were still up. They were probably waiting for her!

Shutting off the engine, Lori took a deep breath to prepare herself. It was ironic. She'd totally blown getting home on time once again— blown it royally—but it all seemed so unimportant now. After what she'd been through, a curfew didn't matter very much.

"Lori! You're home!" Her mother sounded tense when she opened the front door. In the living room, Lori's father looked up from the chair he was sitting in. He flicked off the TV with the remote control and shot Lori a stern look.

"So? What's the excuse this time?" he asked grimly.

Lori couldn't help the smile that crept across her face. "Would you believe, Danielle and I caught the people who were doing the robberies at the mall?"

With that Lori launched into the whole story as her stunned parents drank in every word.

"And then I pulled the lever, and in two minutes—or that's what it felt like anyway—there were at least a dozen policemen there! The robbers were still trying to get the van started, but Danielle really did a number on it."

"Lori! Thank goodness you didn't get hurt!" her mother exclaimed, hugging Lori.

"Well, I'm sure glad I didn't know what was happening at the mall," said her father proudly. "I'd have been tearing my hair out with worry!"

"Anyway, I'm sorry about the curfew. I guess you could say I blew it," Lori said sadly with a resigned shrug. "I tried, but I guess trying wasn't good enough."

"Oh, no, you didn't blow it, Lori," said her father. "If you ever proved how trustworthy you were, it was tonight. You handled yourself beautifully under tremendously difficult circumstances. I don't think we can ask for more than that. And that kind of responsibility deserves its reward.

"As far as I'm concerned, you've earned a

later curfew. If Mom agrees, you can stay out an *hour* later from now on," said her father with a warm smile.

"I agree," said her mother, patting Lori's back gently.

"Thanks a billion!" cried Lori, meaning it from the bottom of her heart. "That means Nick and I can really enjoy Sadie Hawkins night!"

"Get some rest," her mother advised. "It's late."

"Okay, Mom. Good night!"

As she ran up into her room, Lori's heart was pounding in triple time. But this time it was from sheer happiness.

Everything was going to be okay, Danielle just knew it. She walked up the courtroom steps with her father on one side and Don James on the other. In a few minutes Don was going to be cleared of every charge against him—*and it was all because of her*.

The real robbers, including Vince Tripp, were all in custody, and it wouldn't be long before they were serving time behind bars for the crimes they'd committed. Now Merivale was safe again, and best of all, Don was going to be cleared!

A court clerk in a dark blue uniform rapped a gavel and began reading the statement that Danielle had made earlier that morning to the police. Beside her, Don stared nervously at the wooden railing in front of them.

"Danielle Sharp, do you attest to the truth of this statement?" growled the judge from his elevated polished oak desk.

"Yes, your honor, I do," said Danielle.

"Miss Randall? Do you attest to the truth of your statement as well?" the judge repeated, looking at Lori, who sat with her parents two rows back.

"Yes, your honor," said Lori with a smile. "I do."

Turning to look at her cousin, Danielle flashed Lori her thousand-watt smile, and a wink.

"Well, then," declared the judge, "since the court has received these statements and found them to be in proper order, I hereby declare all charges against Donald R. James to be null and void."

A sigh of relief went through the courtroom. Serena Sharp gave Danielle a gentle squeeze around the shoulders. Danielle looked back at her mother fondly. "I'm sorry I lied to you about Don having all that money," she whispered.

"That's all right, darling," said her mother. "Money doesn't matter."

Danielle nearly fainted when she heard her mother say that! By tomorrow Serena Sharp would be the same old snob as ever, of course, but Danielle didn't care. Her mother had uttered the incredible, and that was all that mattered. Her eyes overflowing with happiness, Danielle turned to Don.

"Congratulations," she said shyly.

"Thanks, Red." Don took her hand and squeezed it gently. Danielle felt a rush of warmth make its way from her hand to her toes.

"Don! Congratulations!" Mike Sharp was saying, reaching past the happy lawyer and grabbing Don's hand.

"Thanks, Mr. Sharp. I don't know what I would have done without you. All of you have been just great to me," he said, looking from Danielle's father and mother to Danielle.

Danielle coughed and put her head down. Don was saying that for her parents' sake alone, she was sure. After the way she had treated him about the Sadie Hawkins dance, she was sure he'd never forgive her. Why should he? Danielle didn't think *she'd* be so forgiving under similar circumstances.

"I'm hungry, Red," Don was whispering in her ear now. "Any chance of you and me grabbing a burger or something?"

"Yes! I'd love to!" Could it be? Did he still like her—in that way? If he did, she'd be the happiest girl in the entire universe!

"Mom, Dad—we're going to get a bite, okay?" said Danielle as they were filing out of the courtroom.

"Sure, honey," said her father. "Don, you take care. We'll see you again, I'm sure."

Danielle waved to her parents and to Lori and the Randalls as she and Don made their way to her car.

"If you're still not afraid to be seen with me, we can go to O'Burgers," said Don with a small grin.

Red to the roots of her hair, Danielle turned the key in the lock. "Don—please," she begged, putting her head down in shame. Being reminded of what a disloyal creep she had been was totally humiliating.

"Ah, forget it, Red," Don said gently. "What can I say? You're special to me."

Danielle opened her car door and got in. *You're special to me.* What a beautiful thing to say!

"Oh, Don," she said after they were both in the car and belted up. "I'm so sorry for the way I acted about the dance and everything. The truth is, I'd be proud to show up at Sadie Hawkins with you."

Don arched an eyebrow. "Even if your fancy friends still think I'm a lowlife?"

"Anybody who thinks you're low is crazy," Danielle declared, pushing her key into the ignition.

"Wait a minute, Red. Not so fast," Don said, putting his hand over hers.

Danielle shot him a puzzled look. "What?"

she asked, her green eyes drinking him in thirstily.

Don unfastened his seat belt and put his arm over her shoulder and pulled her gently toward him.

"This is for you," he whispered in her ear. "Just to show you I'm not mad anymore."

Then he reached out and pulled her toward him with his strong arms. And he kissed her on the lips, tenderly at first, then passionately. "Oh, Don," Danielle whispered gratefully.

"Shhhh—don't say anything." Then he silenced her with another kiss. Danielle knew at that moment that she was definitely the happiest girl in the entire universe.

CHAPTER SIXTEEN

"It was his teeth, Lor! Can you believe it!" Patsy Donovan's voice on the phone was full of joy and sheer relief.

Sitting in her bathrobe, her hair in curlers, Lori drank in every word Patsy was saying.

"He was having dental work done and he was embarrassed." Patsy went on with a happy sigh. "Oh, Lor—he's so great—"

Obviously everything had cleared up between Patsy and Irv. Lori reached across her desk and found the peach nail polish she wanted to put on that night. "That's fantastic, Patsy!" she said. "But I knew he liked you all along."

"You were right," Patsy replied. "Oh, Lori, you're such a genius."

"Just call me Lori Einstein. But honestly, anybody could tell Irv adores you just by the look on his face when you walk into a room."

"Oh, and he's so romantic, Lori. Guess where he's taking me tonight?"

"Where, Pats?" asked Lori, balancing the phone on her shoulder so she could put a coat of polish on.

"Bowling."

"Bowling?" Lori chuckled.

"That's what we did the first time we got together, when we were just friends. Well, I know you must need to get ready for Sadie Hawkins. Are you going to Rob Matthews's party?"

"Yup!" Lori said happily. "And my parents rolled back my curfew too! I get to stay out till one."

"Lori, that's great!" cried Patsy. "Oh, isn't life beautiful?"

"I can't argue with that." Lori laughed into the phone. The peach polish was going to look fantastic with her formal gown.

"Well, have fun tonight," said Patsy. "I'll come over tomorrow to find out how it went, okay?"

"Okay," Lori replied. "But not too early, okay? I'm probably going to sleep late."

Lori put down the phone and looked around her room. Her dress was hanging behind the closet door; her nail polish was drying. She was going to spritz herself with the cologne Nick had given her and have one of the happiest nights of her entire life!

*   *   *

"Lori, hi!" Danielle stopped putting out punch glasses for a moment to call to her beautiful blond cousin. On Lori's arm was Atwood's own star quarterback. "Hi, Nick!"

"Lori, you look fabulous! I love your dress," cried Danielle, planting a quick kiss on her cousin's cheek.

"You don't look so bad yourself," Lori teased. Danielle's strapless electric-blue formal clung to her figure and revealed every perfect curve.

"Thanks," Danielle replied as modestly as she could manage. "Being on the dance committee, you know, I thought I should look good."

"Where's Don?" Nick asked, being friendly. "Is he coming?"

"Oh—well, yes and no," Danielle explained. But before she could finish, Heather Barron burst into the hall on the arm of Rob Matthews. Behind her was Ashley Shepard and her date and Teresa Woods and Ben Frye.

"Danielle! That dress is gorgeous!" Hard-to-please Heather Barron meant every word, Danielle could tell.

"Thanks," Danielle said sweetly.

The band started playing and Nick turned to Lori with a grin. "Gee, I wish someone would ask me to dance—"

"Okay, Hobart, I can take a hint. See you later, everyone."

"Bye, you two," Danielle called after them. Nick and Lori were really a great couple. She hadn't been able to appreciate that at first, but seeing them together the past few months had changed her mind.

"Where's your date, Danielle?" Heather wanted to know.

"Oh, on his way, I suppose."

"Don't guess," said Ashley Shepard, gazing out at the entrance. "Here he is now! And look what *he's* wearing!"

As if on cue, Don James strode through the door wearing jeans and his leather jacket, the collar pulled up.

"Don!" cried Danielle and waved just as the ticket taker caught up to him. "So—that's all the punch glasses," she said to Teresa. "Jane Haggerty is handling the spoons. The punch is all ready to go, and I'm off!" said Danielle.

"What?" a shocked Teresa cried.

"See you in a minute." With a giggle, Danielle disappeared into the ladies' room. Minutes later she came out in a pair of black jeans and a black leather jacket of her own. "Well, everybody. Have a great time!" she announced, taking Don's arm and strutting out the door with him.

With a dramatic wave to everyone piling in the door, Danielle jumped onto the back of Don's Harley and Don kicked the bike into action.

Her gorgeous red hair floated behind her as they roared away from Atwood Academy toward the mall. Don was going to give her a Star Command lesson—and then they were just going to hang out!